UNWIN HYMAN SHORT STORIES

DREAMS AND RESOLUTIONS

D1740553

**INCLUDING
FOLLOW ON
ACTIVITIES**

EDITED BY ROY BLATCHFORD

Published in 1988 by
Unwin Hyman Limited
15/17 Broadwick Street
London W1V 1FP

British Library Cataloguing in Publication Data
Dreams and Resolutions
  1. Short stories in English. 1900 —
Anthologies — For schools.
  I. Blatchford, Roy.
823'.01'08 [FS]

  ISBN 0–7135–2841–9

Cover illustration by Simon Morley
Series cover design by Iain Lanyon

Typeset in Great Britain by TJB Photosetting Ltd, South Witham,
Lincolnshire

Printed in Great Britain by Billing & Sons Ltd., Worcester

CONTENTS   *Page*

Introduction by Roy Blatchford

Introduction

Fiction has always been a major resource for teachers and students involved in the study of language and literature. Perhaps its most important contribution has been the enjoyment and pleasure that readers gain. Equally, fiction has been used because of its power to engage attention and the imagination, and give shape to personal experiences and expectations.

Many of the issues we wish to discuss with students are complex, challenging and probing. Reading fiction provides a chance to consider and reflect on them from a distance, before moving into the realm of personal experience and opinion. Fiction also offers a wealth of models of writing and expression that can be used to assist students in their own writing.

The aim of this collection is to provide a resource for students studying GCSE English and English Literature and Standard Grade English. The stories have been selected first and foremost because they are fine examples of the short story genre, and are perhaps best enjoyed when read aloud and shared with a group of students. They also offer opportunities to talk and write about issues that are of concern and relevance to young people.

Certain ideas and themes recur in the stories in *Dreams And Resolutions*: conflict between parents and their children, raw prejudice, the power of memories, the impressionable young mind, the eternal struggle between the sexes. But what unites the stories is that central to each one is some kind of 'meeting' which has a profound effect on one or more of the characters. In turn, the impact of these fictional meetings passes through to the reader's imagination. As Linda Cookson observes in her personal essay:

'Short stories have much more in common with poetry than with novels. Partly that's because of their compactness, and the way in which they're so tightly controlled. Partly it's because they very often only focus on a single place or moment in time. But it also, I think, has something to do with the very intense *emotional* appeal that a short story can make to the reader'.

It is both the enjoyment and the challenge for the reader of short stories that s/he is drawn emotionally into the writer's world. Here we engage with characters and places glimpsed by an author as in a snapshot.

Opening the collection is a beautifully crafted and quietly unnerving tale 'Three Resolutions To One Kashmiri Encounter' which, as the title hints, offers the reader a choice of endings. The story sets the agenda of the volume with its bringing together of two characters, a meeting which is to have a lasting effect on at least one of them. Linda Cookson's 'Fireflies' and Flannery O'Connor's 'The Life You Save May Be Your Own' focus on equally significant encounters, though the contexts, locations and central figures are very different.

Meetings which occur during childhood and the memories of these (which last long into adulthood) lie at the heart of two sensitively cast narratives 'Talks With My Uncle Moro' and 'The Scythe', both of which are previously unpublished. Their warm evocation of childhood and nostalgia for days past have an instant appeal.

There are illuminating parallels to be drawn between 'He Said...', 'A Father' and 'Marriage Is A Private Affair', where meetings between parents and children rapidly develop into furious, even violent, confrontation. The fact that in all three stories the 'children' are young adults in their own right serves merely to remind us of the perennial nature of conflicting generations. Resolutions — of a kind — are presented for the reader to dwell on....and perhaps challenge.

'Sphinxes' is a captivating, enigmatic, perhaps humorous tale which pitches the individual against the anonymous forces of the State, while in 'A Drive In The Country' (with its distinct echoes of *Brighton Rock*) Graham Greene's characteristically racy narrative and storytelling instincts are much in evidence.

'Three Dreams In A Desert' deliberately concludes the volume, partly with its echoing of the opening 'Three Resolutions' and partly because it has a futuristic, visionary quality in both style and content. Moreover, it pulls together in an allegorical setting the themes of prejudice and equality found throughout these eleven stories.

In all cases, stories must stand or fall on their ability to engage the reader. Indeed, as Giles Gordon's personal essay reminds us:

'Once written and published, stories cease to be the property of their writers. They belong to each and every reader, to interpret as they will and can. Authors are readers, readers authors — a continuum. The writer has no identity without the reader'.

The range of 'Follow On' activities is designed to present a variety of talking and writing assignments that will help students to gain in confidence and competence at using language effectively in any context. They also offer a range of approaches which will help students of *all* abilities, whether in building up a coursework folder or in preparing for essays written under examination conditions. More specifically, the activities aim to encourage students to:
 – work independently and collaboratively
 – consider:
   the short story as a genre
   language and style of a writer
   structure and development of plot

development of character
setting
- examine the writer's viewpoint and intentions
- respond critically and imaginatively to the stories, orally and in writing
- read a variety of texts, including quite difficult ones
- read more widely

One important footnote: the activities are divided under three broad headings:

Before Reading – enabling the student to anticipate and speculate about what is going to happen.

During Reading – building up a picture of what is going on and what may happen next.

After Reading – allowing time to reflect on the setting, events, characters, issues and themes within the stories; giving opportunities for discussion, and for personal, critical and discursive writing.

Teachers using the collection are therefore recommended to preview the 'Follow On' section before reading the stories with students.

Roy Blatchford

GILES GORDON

Three Resolutions To One Kashmiri Encounter

An Arid Title For A Human Incident

That morning I took a day tour in what was described in the brochure as a luxury coach from Srinagar — 'the russet-coloured, autumnal-smelling capital of Kashmir in the heady north of India' — to Gulmarg, 'the meadow of flowers', fifty-one kilometres away and 2,590 metres up in the Himalayas.

The coach from Srinagar, a ravishing city built on water, as colourful and chaotic as its name is impossible to pronounce, passed through lush countryside. On both sides of the straight, well-surfaced roads were paddy fields — many of them saturated with water, being worked on more often than not by women of all ages in floral pyjama outfits, the female national dress of Kashmir — and avenues of poplars. High up in the mountains was snow which, even in the last week of April, defied all efforts by the blazing sun to dislodge it. From the distance, the white on the peaks looked glossy and sleek like the coats of well-tended ponies.

We stopped for a ten-minute break at Tangmarg, a mountain village and another beauty spot five and a half kilometres from the higher Gulmarg. I suspect the coach and its driver required a breather before undertaking the final ascent, the road from Tangmarg being narrow, circuitous and hazardous.

I say 'final ascent' — final, that is, for vehicles, after which ponies and sledges, rope-tow and chair lift take over. The ski lifts were not in use, as on the lower slopes the snow had been melting for a couple of weeks, causing the rivers and streams to pour their brown and grey waters in torrents through the Kashmir valley. I didn't, at Tangmarg, avail myself of a cup of tea or coffee, as passengers were invited to do and most of the Indian families and couples did, preferring to wander up and down the single street of the village, looking at the bazaar and what through their open fronts the shops and stalls had to offer, and observe the mountain people. They were slim and wiry, taller and less stocky than the Nepalese, their faces without any spare flesh, tough, sun-beaten, snow-beaten: the countenance of a mountain people in the heart of Asia, further north than Tibet. They looked more Oriental than Indian. Visitors — five or six other coaches were parked in front of the Tourist Reception building in the middle of the village — mingled with the villagers. There was a whirl of activity. It was suddenly as if Tangmarg were a melting pot, the centre of the world. A stage had been animated.

A middle-aged man, with some distinction in his features and a dignified manner, was standing beside me, speaking to me. They tread so softly, so used are they to the terrain and the mountains, that you don't hear them approach. In good English — not at all with an Indian accent — he asked if I wouldn't prefer to leave the coach here and rejoin it on its return journey in the later afternoon, and he would guide me up the mountains, or wherever in the area I would like to go. I thanked him for his offer but declined.

'Only for six miles,' he said, and I was quietly pleased that he'd implied as great a mileage as that as being a short trek. He must have assumed I was more fit than I felt. The air up here made me tire easily and frequently search for breath. Again I declined, shaking my head.

'Let me come with you anyway,' he said, all the while absolutely and without difficulty managing to retain his character, individuality, dignity. There are beggars and beggars in India, indeed at times it seems both that they dominate the country and that the country has its being to enable them to beg, but not here in the exhilarating mountain air of Kashmir, gateway to heaven. There was, in this man, no element of grovelling, hardly even of importuning. He was his own master. His proposal was made entirely for my good. If I turned him down I was the loser.

'No, I prefer to go on my own,' I said. 'I'm sorry.' He seemed to accept my decision but showed no sign of being about to walk away, to solicit some other travellers. He began to tell me the names and heights of the local mountains, pointing them out to me, taking his time both as if to ensure I would manage to retain the information in my head and to prolong our encounter for its own sake. Besides, the *mountains* were hardly in a hurry. Harmukh and Ferozepur, Sunset Peaks and Apharwat Ridge. He kept the name and height of the last mountain, the mightiest of them all, to the end, producing it as if he'd just created the thing and I was the first to learn of his triumph: Nanga Parbat, 26,660 feet. How could I respond? Is *that* Nanga Parbat? Some height.

I said nothing, just looked. Still he stood by me, though it was as if I stood by him, as if I had sought him out and insisted on being with him. Somehow I felt it impossible — too discourteous to a fellow human being — to walk away from him. Besides, he might have followed me, though I didn't believe he would have done. And where could I have gone? Only up or down the village street, the street that was his village, his home. In my mind I urged the coach driver to sound his horn to indicate that we should all return to the vehicle, that it was about to move off and on to Gulmarg.

In a still, quiet voice — as if he was confiding in me — he began to talk again. 'Last year my wife died and I was left to bring up our three children. For six months one of them was in hospital, with a badly injured leg.' He paused, before going on. 'There is hardly any work here, in Tangmarg.'

I felt unable to say anything; or, rather, anything I might have said could only sound gratuitous, insensitive. He then said, so I understood it, that one rice meal a day for four people — and the children had big appetites — cost one rupee, which I'd have thought a little on the high side (a few pence) but hardly began to invalidate the point he was making. No work, no money, no food.

The horn of the coach went and I excused myself from him, saying that I hoped things got better for him, and quickly. I looked him in the eyes and nodded solemnly, as if to make it plain — in spite of having failed to provide him with employment and a rupee or two — that I wished him well. As if he could care. Somehow he managed neither to accept nor acknowledge my farewell, my intended affirmation of good will in the face of the facts, nor to reject it. He allowed me to go.

Inside myself, I had panicked — for the sake of a coin or two — and felt disgusted. I was filled with a fluttering self-loathing. As the coach moved away, I watched him walking slowly down the street, his body built for survival, his head lowered a little in the direction of the ground.

Six hours later the coach returned. I'd prayed that it wouldn't halt at Tangmarg but it did, as in the morning on the way up. During the day, walking miles in the relentless and joyous air of the mountains, I found that my encounter with the man at Tangmarg kept coming back to me, nagged and fretted at the edges of my mind. Because I hadn't provided him with work, even for a short period of time, an hour or two, he had no money and therefore couldn't buy rice for his children and himself. On the other hand, so I tried to rationalize, I was hardly the only person he could have asked. There had been thirty or forty coaches at Gulmarg, and they all must have stopped at Tangmarg in the morning on the upward climb. I didn't owe the man a living, or no more than anyone else did. I wasn't his keeper. Our encounter had been a chance one. Why then should I have felt so strongly that I was the only person he asked, that because of that I was responsible for his well-being and that of his family? Had he not an obligation to go on asking people if they'd like to use his services until someone responded in the affirmative?

I remained in the overheated and airless coach at Tangmarg on the way back because I could see him from where the vehicle was parked, sitting on the ground in front of a shop, his hands wrapped around his raised knees. He didn't seem to belong to the shop, either to be working there or to be purchasing something from it. How could he have done, if he'd no money? Yet he seemed aware of the conversation going on between the man behind the counter and the person he was chatting to on the other side, in the street.

He looked no more hopeful or dejected than he had in the morning. It was as if the day had passed him by. He may have noticed my coach, realized that it was the one I arrived on in the morning, but he gave no indication of looking or of seeing, of being interested or concerned. Besides, most of these coaches looked pretty alike. He had troubled my mind but I doubted whether I had his, that my rejection of his services and of him had remained with him for longer than the moment of rejection had taken. The irony, of course, was that it was he who had wanted, needed something from me, not me from him.

Ten minutes later the coach started up, began to move from its parking place and down the hill on the last stage of its journey back to Srinagar. For as long as he was in view I watched from behind the curtain of my window seat. He didn't look up.

Six hours later, when the sun was beginning to descend towards and behind the mountains and what had been the excited, frenetic atmosphere of Gulmarg was growing wistful, contemplative, the coach began its return journey. As in the morning, on the way out, it stopped at Tangmarg. During the bright and crisp and peaceful hours of the day, up above the valley, watching the men of the mountains pull visitors on sledges up snowy slopes and in and out of fir and pine forests, my meeting of the morning with the would-be guide of Tangmarg kept coming back to me, worrying at my mind. Especially did it do so when I was eating a skilfully cooked egg *paratha* and drinking a cup of steaming black tea at a refreshment hut high up in the mountains. It was an image, the meeting between us, which I couldn't with a clear conscience — with any conscience at all — expel from my mind. Had the man been sycophantically crawling, simply for alms (*baksheesh*, a tip or reward) as in the case with the majority of the beggars of India, then I would have had no compunction in not slipping him a coin. After all, he was able-bodied and thus able to work — eager to work. Both, I suspected, for the satisfaction of the work itself and for the income it would bring him. To have given him a rupee or two would have made no noticeable difference to my pocket. To him and his dependents it would have meant sustenance for a day or even two.

I alighted from the coach at Tangmarg with the other passengers but I didn't filter slowly into the café or to one of the stalls as most of them did. I looked about for my man, the man of the morning, having decided before arriving back that if he was in the street and I saw him I would give him two rupees. One which I should have given him in the morning, the other to appease my conscience.

I saw him almost as soon as I had stepped from the coach, coming up the street, in nearly the same place he'd been in the morning when I saw him go down when the coach left. He wasn't looking up, he wasn't particularly looking up. He didn't give the impression of expecting to see someone he knew. Yet there was a kind of purposefulness about his progress, as if he wasn't proceeding up the street just to pass the time, to do something, that he wasn't walking merely for the sake of walking but that he had an objective in mind.

Though he was only a few paces from me, I began to move towards him. He looked up when I was close to him, three or four paces away, when he realized that someone was in his path. His eyes, which were both observant and bright yet somehow defeated, reconciled to the sorrows of life, of his life, registered no particular recognition of me; but neither the opposite. Our eyes met. I was neither stranger nor friend, enemy or ally.

'I wanted to thank you,' I said, 'for what you told me this morning.' The expression on his face didn't alter. 'About the mountains. Their names. Heights. Very interesting.'

I stopped. What more could I say, confronted with his silence, his lack of communication? I'd imagined he'd say something but he didn't. What could there have been for him to say? Yet he didn't seem to be judging me, despising me, which made it more difficult.

I held out my hand to him. His was raised to meet mine, to take the money. Without looking down to see how much it was, he took the note, then withdrew his hand.

'Thank you,' he said; and then once more, as if he wasn't sure that he'd uttered the words the first time. There was a slow, grateful nod of the head before he broke away and walked around me and continued up the street to wherever he'd been going.

Six hours later, by the time the coach began its return journey to Srinagar, I had resolved upon a course of action. The day, for me, had been an unusually satisfying one. Unusually so, because I'm not regularly given to wandering about the snow-covered Himalayas. I'd had no preconceptions as to how I'd feel up there, higher than I'd ever been, how free and irresponsible yet somehow in command of my destiny. Close to, with the sun grinning down on their great flanks, the mountains looked as if hewn from marble. The local men wearing multi-coloured knitted caps and woollen jumpers, dragged docile Indians on holiday up the slopes on sledges, into and amidst forests of vast firs. Children and sometimes adults pelted each other laboriously with snowballs, at times giggling solemnly as if Indians shouldn't indulge themselves as abandonedly as this. A red-turbaned Sikh thundered along a path on a white pony, followed at a proper distance by his wife and two daughters on grey ponies. On the lower levels the snow was melting fast, as if a whole winter's downpour felt obliged to vacate itself in one afternoon when confronted by incipient spring. Water flooded down springy, grassy fields translating them into water meadows. Huge black crows cackled and cawed, glided from tree to snow, snow to tree, black against white.

Against this heightened atmosphere — in both senses, every sense — my unproductive (from his point of view) meeting with the man at Tangmarg in the morning lay at the back of my mind, tingeing my exultation in the present with irritation and dissatisfaction. Had the man begged, asked for alms, would I have given? After he'd told me his tale, assuming it was the same tale, I suspect I would. Not that, needing every coin and note and travellers' cheque I had with me in India, I'm in the habit of giving to beggars but because I believed the man implicitly, respected his self-respect and was grateful *not* to have him accompany me. I would have paid him so that I could be alone. All this, as I say, had he begged and importuned. But he didn't, he asked only to accompany me, to be my guide or companion for a period.

Near the end of the afternoon, before it was time to return to the coach, I had something tasty to eat and a glass of coffee with goat's milk at a café high up above the chair-lift wires. I took pleasure in watching the steam from the coffee rise upwards and look quite dark, almost opaque against the snow before turning translucent again and evaporating. Lurching downwards on the chair lift — above snow, trees, torrents of water, birds, people — I resolved what to do if the coach stopped at Tangmarg, as I felt pretty certain it would as Indians like their stops for tea or coffee. I even felt pleased with myself in anticipation.

As the coach parked in the centre of the village, the same spot as in the morning, alongside three other returning coaches, and with both villagers and visitors milling about, though without the excited tension, the expectancy of the morning, I at once saw my man. He was standing by a stall, a shop slightly down the sloping street from where the coach was. I hoped he wouldn't disappear before I could get out of the vehicle but, sitting near the back as I was, I was obliged to let the people in front alight first.

He was in the same place when I stepped out. I hurried over to him and stood there, smiling.

'Hallo,' I said.

'Sir,' he said, rather stiffly; 'sir', rather than the more usual 'sahib'.

I felt slightly hurt that he wasn't immediately more forthcoming, more friendly. *Presumably* he recognized me, remembered.

'Look,' I said, 'I'd like you to have this,' and held out to him the five-rupee note which I'd been clutching in my hand for half an hour or more. He looked down at it.

'No, sir,' he said, peering into my eyes. 'I asked you this morning if you'd employ me, and you wouldn't.' Then, without a pause: 'How did you like Gulmarg?'

'I...liked it...a lot,' I said, well aware of the feebleness of my response in the face of his rejection of my money, and of me.

'Yes, it is very beautiful,' he said.

'Very beautiful,' I repeated.

He walked away, up the street. Slowly I returned to the coach, crushing the note in my hand. There was little point in hurrying as the vehicle wouldn't be leaving until everyone had had their tea or coffee.

GILES GORDON

*P*ersonal Essay

I wasn't aware, particularly, that I was lazy at school, but clearly I was. I failed to pass sufficient of the necessary examinations to advance to further education, and upon leaving school, obtained a menial job in the advertising department of a publishing house in Edinburgh. In those days, the late 1950s, it was still reasonably easy for the unqualified but enthusiastic to procure jobs. I was, and still am really, passionate about the writing and making of books, and I quickly picked up the business of publishing.

After a few years, I left Edinburgh to seek my fortune in London. I had a number of editorial jobs, culminating in becoming editorial director of Victor Gollancz Ltd where, more or less, I could take on any manuscript I wanted. Being a publisher is a dangerous boost to the individual's ego. You begin to believe your judgement is somehow significant.

At the same time, I was writing novels, and found it virtually impossible (if I was to have a private life) to combine publishing and writing. I was lucky enough to be offered a job as a literary agent where I could work three days a week, looking after the professional lives of writers whose work I admired, and write my own books the rest of the time.

With six novels and three collections of short stories published, I realised — all of a sudden, just like that — that I had run out of material, inspiration. It was a terrible shock. Lyric poets often give up writing poetry by the time they are in their thirties, when novelists are supposed to be beginning. 60,000 words — most novels are not shorter — is a long haul, and few people have the stamina, the verbal energy and expertise, let alone the experience of life's haphazard patchwork quilt to produce novels of sophistication, complexity, accuracy and truth when they are younger than thirty. And here was me, aged thirty-nine, claiming to have shot my bolt.

I was lucky enough to work for a small organisation (I still do: I could not live off my writing) which was and is sympathetic to the needs and desires of the individual. I asked if I could, in 1980, have six months' sabbatical, and I was granted it. I regarded it as my reward for having missed university, and certainly I would make the most of it. I first worked for a month on a kibbutz in Israel (I'd never worked harder) and then had ten weeks in India. When there, I wrote very little — 'fiction' that is; I kept detailed notebooks, writing thousands of words most days – instead 'experienced life', something you too easily forget about when earning your living.

Nearly a decade has passed since then, and I have not written another novel. For me, 'the novel' is essentially a 19th century form, those wonderful slabs or doorstops of narrative, of tuppence coloured characters in motion. Today television does, for better or for worse, what the novel did. Fiction has had to find a new purpose, a reason to exist. There is little artistic point in rewriting, say, Dickens for today.

To me, the experience of living in Britain in the 1980s can most satisfyingly be expressed in short fictional form, in short stories — though I'm chary of using that expression since the novelist B.S. Johnson pronounced that 'telling stories is telling lies'. Lies can, on occasion, be useful, and stories are fun, intriguing and beguiling.

'Three Resolutions to One Kashmiri Encounter' is set in India but the narrator — I confess he is me — is obviously British. A short story should, I believe, be a challenge for the writer at least as much as for the reader. If the writer isn't stretched, why should the reader give him or her the privilege of his or her time?

I wanted the story to work on a number of levels. First, as it is set in foreign parts – Kashmir – an element of travelogue, of exoticism, of different climate and culture has to be present. The reader, painlessly, should have a 'feel' of the place. Second, it should tell a story, whether or not that story is a 'lie'. Did it happen to the author? (Yes, it did.) And if it did, or didn't, is that remotely important to the story, whether it works on its own terms or doesn't? I say it happened, and I believe it did. But, as the deliberately solemn title states, there are *three* resolutions. Three choices, in fact. Only one of them — or maybe none — could have happened. Which do you, as reader, think it was?

You may not believe this but I swear it's true: I cannot remember, eight years on. The incident as recounted in the story more or less happened, happened more or less as I have written it. Much of it — the anxiety, the fear, the guilt, the angst — takes place in the narrator's mind. What happened to me in Tangmarg that day ceased to be part of my life, my experience as soon as I had distilled it, reinvented it, reinterpreted it as fiction. That is the point. The incident hadn't happened, in reality. The story existed, the story is neither more nor less than the construct of words, sentences, paragraphs I have put together.

When invited to introduce my story for this collection, I had to go back and reread it, not having done so since it was originally published. The story no longer remotely belonged to me. I neither recognised it, nor remembered what would happen. Once written and published, stories cease to be the property of their writers. They belong to each and every reader, to interpret as they will and can. Authors are readers, readers authors — a continuum. The writer has no identity without the reader.

Besides which — and this, no doubt, is substantially why I failed my school exams — I have a lousy memory. It is easier, difficult though it is, to conjure fiction than to document fact. I believe, and hope you do, that fiction is usually closer to life as we experience it, to reality.

FLANNERY O'CONNOR

The Life You Save May Be Your Own

The old woman and her daughter were sitting on their porch when Mr. Shiftlet came up their road for the first time. The old woman slid to the edge of her chair and leaned forward, shading her eyes from the piercing sunset with her hand. The daughter could not see far in front of her and continued to play with her fingers. Although the old woman lived in this desolate spot with only her daughter and she had never seen Mr. Shiftlet before, she could tell, even from a distance, that he was a tramp and no one to be afraid of. His left coat sleeve was folded up to show there was only half an arm in it and his gaunt figure listed slightly to the side as if the breeze were pushing him. He had on a black town suit and a brown felt hat that was turned up in the front and down in the back and he carried a tin tool box by a handle. He came on, at an amble, up her road, his face turned toward the sun which appeared to be balancing itself on the peak of a small mountain.

The old woman didn't change her position until he was almost into her yard; then she rose with one hand fisted on her hip. The daughter, a large girl in a short blue organdy dress, saw him all at once and jumped up and began to stamp and point and make excited speechless sounds.

Mr. Shiftlet stopped just inside the yard and set his box on the ground and tipped his hat at her as if she were not in the least afflicted; then he turned toward the old woman and swung the hat all the way off. He had long black slick hair that hung from a part in the middle to beyond the tips of his ears on either side. His face descended in forehead for more than half its length and ended suddenly with his features just balanced over a jutting steel-trap jaw. He seemed to be a young man but he had a look of composed dissatisfaction as if he understood life thoroughly.

'Good evening,' the old woman said. She was about the size of a cedar fence post and she had a man's gray hat pulled down low over her head.

The tramp stood looking at her and didn't answer. He turned his back and faced the sunset. He swung both his whole and his short arm up slowly so that they indicated an expanse of sky and his figure formed a crooked cross. The old woman watched him with her arms folded across her chest as if she were the owner of the sun, and the daughter watched, her head thrust forward and her fat helpless hands hanging at the wrists. She had long pink-gold hair and eyes as blue as peacock's neck.

He held the pose for almost fifty seconds and then he picked up his box and came on to the porch and dropped down on the bottom step. 'Lady,' he said in a firm nasal voice, 'I'd give a fortune to live where I could see me a sun do that every evening.'

'Does it every evening,' the old woman said and sat back down. The daughter sat down too and watched him with a cautious sly look as if he were a bird that had come up very close. He leaned to one side, rooting in his pants pocket, and in a second he brought out a package of chewing gum and offered her a piece. She took it and unpeeled it and began to chew without taking her eyes off him. He offered the old woman a piece but she only raised her upper lip to indicate she had no teeth.

Mr. Shiftlet's pale sharp glance had already passed over everything in the yard—the pump near the corner of the house and the big fig tree that three or four chickens were preparing to roost in—and had moved to a shed where he saw the square rusted back of an automobile. 'You ladies drive?' he asked.

'That car ain't run in fifteen year,' the old woman said. 'The day my husband died, it quit running.'

'Nothing is like it used to be, lady,' he said. 'The world is almost rotten.'

'That's right,' the old woman said. 'You from around here?'

'Name Tom T. Shiftlet,' he murmured, looking at the tires.

'I'm pleased to meet you,' the old woman said. 'Name Lucynell Crater and daughter Lucynell Crater. What you doing around here, Mr. Shiftlet?'

He judged the car to be about a 1928 or '29 Ford. 'Lady,' he said, and turned and gave her his full attention, 'lemme tell you something. There's one of these doctors in Atlanta that's taken a knife and cut the human heart—the human heart,' he repeated, leaning forward, 'out of a man's chest and held it in his hand,' and he held his hand out, palm up, as if it were slightly weighted with the human heart, 'and studied it like it was a day-old chicken, and lady,' he said, allowing a long significant pause in which his head slid forward and his clay-colored eyes brightened,' he don't know no more about it than you or me.'

'That's right,' the old woman said.

'Why, if he was to take that knife and cut into every corner of it, he still wouldn't know no more than you or me. What you want to bet?'

'Nothing,' the old woman said wisely. 'Where you come from, Mr. Shiftlet?'

He didn't answer. He reached into his pocket and brought out a sack of tobacco and a package of cigarette papers and rolled himself a cigarette, expertly with one hand, and attached it in a hanging position to his upper lip. Then he took a box of wooden matches from his pocket and struck one on his shoe. He held the burning match as if he were studying the mystery of flame while it traveled dangerously toward his skin. The daughter began to make loud noises and to point to his hand and shake her finger at him, but when the flame was just before touching him, he leaned down with his hand cupped over it as if he were going to set fire to his nose and lit the cigarette.

15

He flipped away the dead match and blew a stream of gray into the evening. A sly look came over his face. 'Lady,' he said, 'nowadays, people'll do anything anyways. I can tell you my name is Tom T. Shiftlet and I come from Tarwater, Tennessee, but you never have seen me before: how you know I ain't lying? How you know my name ain't Aaron Sparks, lady, and I come from Singleberry, Georgia, or how you know it's not George Speeds and I come from Lucy, Alabama, or how you know I ain't Thompson Bright from Toolafalls, Mississippi?'

'I don't know nothing about you,' the old woman muttered, irked.

'Lady,' he said, 'people don't care how they lie. Maybe the best I can tell you is, I'm a man; but listen lady,' he said and paused and made his tone more ominous still, 'what is a man?'

The old woman began to gum a seed. 'What you carry in that tin box, Mr. Shiftlet?' she asked.

'Tools,' he said, put back. 'I'm a carpenter.'

'Well, if you come out here to work, I'll be able to feed you and give you a place to sleep but I can't pay. I'll tell you that before you begin,' she said.

There was no answer at once and no particular expression on his face. He leaned back against the two-by-four that helped support the porch roof. 'Lady,' he said slowly, 'there's some men that some things mean more to them than money.' The old woman rocked without comment and the daughter watched the trigger that moved up and down in his neck. He told the old woman then that all most people were interested in was money, but he asked what a man was made for. He asked her if a man was made for money, or what. He asked her what she thought she was made for but she didn't answer, she only sat rocking and wondered if a one-armed man could put a new roof on her garden house. He asked a lot of questions that she didn't answer. He told her that he was twenty-eight years old and had lived a varied life. He had been a gospel singer, a foreman on the railroad, an assistant in an under-taking parlor, and he had come over the radio for three months with Uncle Roy and his Red Creek Wranglers. He said he had fought and bled in the Arm Service of his country and visited every foreign land and that everywhere he had seen

16

people that didn't care if they did a thing one way or another. He said he hadn't been raised thataway.

A fat yellow moon appeared in the branches of the fig tree as if it were going to roost there with the chickens. He said that a man had to escape to the country to see the world whole and that he wished he lived in a desolate place like this where he could see the sun go down every evening like God made it to do.

'Are you married or are you single?' the old woman asked.

There was a long silence. 'Lady,' he asked finally, 'where would you find you an innocent woman today? I wouldn't have any of this trash I could just pick up.'

The daughter was leaning very far down, hanging her head almost between her knees, watching him through a triangular door she had made in her overturned hair; and she suddenly fell in a heap on the floor and began to whimper. Mr. Shiftlet straightened her out and helped her get back in the chair.

'Is she your baby girl?' he asked.

'My only,' the old woman said, 'and she's the sweetest girl in the world. I wouldn't give her up for nothing on earth. She's smart too. She can sweep the floor, cook, wash, feed the chickens, and hoe. I wouldn't give her up for a casket of jewels.'

'No,' he said kindly, 'don't ever let any man take her away from you.'

'Any man come after her,' the old woman said, 'I'll have to stay around the place.'

Mr. Shiftlet's eye in the darkness was focused on a part of the automobile bumper that glittered in the distance. 'Lady,' he said, jerking his short arm up as if he could point with it to her house and yard and pump, 'there ain't a broken thing on this plantation that I couldn't fix for you, one-arm jackleg or not. I'm a man,' he said with a sullen dignity, 'even if I ain't a whole one. I got,' he said, tapping his knuckles on the floor to emphasize the immensity of what he was going to say, 'a moral intelligence!' and his face pierced out of the darkness into a shaft of doorlight and he stared at her as if he were astonished himself at this impossible truth.

The old woman was not impressed with the phrase. 'I told you you could hang around and work for food,' she said, 'if you don't mind sleeping in that car yonder.'

'Why listen, Lady,' he said with a grin of delight, 'the monks of old slept in their coffins!'

'They wasn't as advanced as we are,' the old woman said.

The next morning he began on the roof of the garden house while Lucynell, the daughter, sat on a rock and watched him work. He had not been around a week before the change he had made in the place was apparent. He had patched the front and back steps, built a new hog pen, restored a fence, and taught Lucynell, who was completely deaf and had never said a word in her life, to say the word 'bird.' The big rosy-faced girl followed him everywhere, saying 'Burrttddt ddbirrrttdt,' and clapping her hands. The old woman watched from a distance, secretly pleased. She was ravenous for a son-in-law.

Mr. Shiftlet slept on the hard narrow back seat of the car with his feet out the side window. He had his razor and can of water on a crate that served him as a bedside table and he put up a piece of mirror against the back glass and kept his coat neatly on a hanger that he hung over one of the windows.

In the evenings he sat on the steps and talked while the old woman and Lucynell rocked violently in their chairs on either side of him. The old woman's three mountains were black against the dark blue sky and were visited off and on by various planets and by the moon after it had left the chickens. Mr. Shiftlet pointed out that the reason he had improved this plantation was because he had taken a personal interest in it. He said he was even going to make the automobile run.

He had raised the hood and studied the mechanism and he said he could tell that the car had been built in the days when cars were really built. You take now, he said, one man puts in one bolt and another man puts in another bolt and another man puts in another bolt so that it's a man for a bolt. That's why you have to pay so much for a car: you're paying all those men. Now if you didn't have to pay but one man, you could get a cheaper car and one that had had a personal interest taken in it, and it would be a better car. The old woman agreed with him that this was so.

Mr. Shiftlet said that the trouble with the world was that

nobody cared, or stopped and took any trouble. He said he never would have been able to teach Lucynell to say a word if he hadn't cared and stopped long enough.

'Teach her to say something else,' the old woman said.

'What you want her to say next?' Mr. Shiftlet asked.

The old woman's smile was broad and toothless and suggestive. 'Teach her to say 'sugarpie,'' she said.

Mr. Shiftlet already knew what was on her mind.

The next day he began to tinker with the automobile and that evening he told her that if she would buy a fan belt, he would be able to make the car run.

The old woman said she would give him the money. 'You see that girl yonder?' she asked, pointing to Lucynell who was sitting on the floor a foot away, watching him, her eyes blue even in the dark. 'If it was ever a man wanted to take her away, I would say, 'No man on earth is going to take that sweet girl of mine away from me!' but if he was to say, 'Lady, I don't want to take her away, I want her right here,' I would say, 'Mister, I don't blame you none. I wouldn't pass up a chance to live in a permanent place and get the sweetest girl in the world myself. You ain't no fool,' I would say.

'How old is she?' Mr. Shiftlet asked casually.

'Fifteen, sixteen,' the old woman said. The girl was nearly thirty but because of her innocence it was impossible to guess.

'It would be a good idea to paint it too,' Mr. Shiftlet remarked. 'You don't want it to rust out.'

'We'll see about that later,' the old woman said.

The next day he walked into town and returned with the parts he needed and a can of gasoline. Late in the afternoon, terrible noises issued from the shed and the old woman rushed out of the house, thinking Lucynell was somewhere having a fit. Lucynell was sitting on a chicken crate, stamping her feet and screaming, 'Burrddttt! bddurrddttt!' but her fuss was drowned out by the car. With a volley of blasts it emerged from the shed, moving in a fierce and stately way. Mr. Shiftlet was in the driver's seat, sitting very erect. He had an expression of serious modesty on his face as if he had just raised the dead.

That night, rocking on the porch, the old woman began her business at once. 'You want you an innocent woman, don't you?' she asked sympathetically. 'You don't want none of this trash.'

'No'm, I don't,' Mr. Shiftlet said.

One that can't talk,' she continued, 'can't sass you back or use foul language. That's the kind for you to have. Right there,' and she pointed to Lucynell sitting cross-legged in her chair, holding both feet in her hands.

'That's right,' he admitted. 'She wouldn't give me any trouble.'

'Saturday,' the old woman said, 'you and her and me can drive into town and get married.'

Mr. Shiftlet eased his position on the steps.

'I can't get married right now,' he said. 'Everything you want to do takes money and I ain't got any.'

'What you need with money?' she asked.

'It takes money,' he said. 'Some people'll do anything anyhow these days, but the way I think, I wouldn't marry no woman that I couldn't take on a trip like she was somebody. I mean take her to a hotel and treat her. I wouldn't marry the Duchesser Windsor,' he said firmly, 'unless I could take her to a hotel and give her something good to eat.'

I was raised thataway and there ain't a thing I can do about it. My old mother taught me how to do.'

'Lucynell don't even know what a hotel is,' the old woman muttered. 'Listen here, Mr. Shiftlet,' she said, sliding forward in her chair, 'you'd be getting a permanent house and a deep well and the most innocent girl in the world. You don't need no money. Lemme tell you something: there ain't any place in the world for a poor disabled friendless drifting man.

The ugly words settled in Mr. Shiftlet's head like a group of buzzards in the top of a tree. He didn't answer at once. He rolled himself a cigarette and lit it and then he said in an even voice, 'Lady, a man is divided into two parts, body and spirit.'

The old woman clamped her gums together.

'A body and a spirit,' he repeated. 'The body, lady, is like a house: It don't go anywhere; but the spirit, lady, is like a automobile: always on the move, always ...'

'Listen, Mr. Shiftlet,' she said, 'my well never goes dry and my house is always warm in the winter and there's no mortgage on a thing about this place. You can go to the court-house and see for yourself. And yonder under that shed is a fine automobile.' She laid the bait carefully. 'You can have it painted by Saturday. I'll pay for the paint.'

In the darkness, Mr. Shiftlet's smile stretched like a weary snake waking up by a fire. After a second he recalled himself and said, 'I'm only saying a man's spirit means more to him than anything else. I would have to take my wife off for the week end without no regards at all for cost. I got to follow where my spirit says to go.'

'I'll give you fifteen dollars for a week-end trip,' the old woman said in a crabbed voice. 'That's the best I can do.'

'That wouldn't hardly pay for more than the gas and the hotel,' he said. 'It wouldn't feed her.'

'Seventeen-fifty,' the old woman said. 'That's all I got so it isn't any use you trying to milk me. You can take a lunch.'

Mr. Shiftlet was deeply hurt by the word 'milk.' He didn't doubt that she had more money sewed up in her mattress but he had already told her he was not interested in her money. 'I'll make that do,' he said and rose and walked off without treating with her further.

On Saturday the three of them drove into town in the car that the paint had barely dried on and Mr. Shiftlet and Lucynell were married in the Ordinary's office while the old woman witnessed. As they came out of the courthouse, Mr. Shiftlet began twisting his neck in his collar. He looked morose and bitter as if he had been insulted while someone held him. 'That didn't satisfy me none,' he said. 'That was just some-thing a woman in an office did, nothing but paper work and blood tests. What do they know about my blood? If they was to take my heart and cut it out,' he said, 'they wouldn't know a thing about me. It didn't satisfy me at all.'

'It satisfied the law,' the old woman said sharply.

'The law,' Mr. Shiftlet said and spit. 'It's the law that don't satisfy me.'

He had painted the car dark green with a yellow band around it just under the windows. The three of them climbed in the front seat and the old woman said, 'Don't Lucynell look pretty? Looks like a baby doll.' Lucynell was dressed up in a

21

white dress that her mother had uprooted from a trunk and there was a Panama hat on her head with a bunch of red wooden cherries on the brim. Every now and then her placid expression was changed by a sly isolated little thought like a shoot of green in the desert. 'You got a prize!' the old woman said.

Mr. Shiftlet didn't even look at her.

They drove back to the house to let the old woman off and pick up the lunch. When they were ready to leave, she stood staring in the window of the car, with her fingers clenched around the glass. Tears began to seep sideways out of her eyes and run along the dirty creases in her face. 'I ain't never been parted with her for two days before,' she said.

Mr. Shiftlet started the motor.

'And I wouldn't let no man have her but you because I seen you would do right. Good-by, Sugarbaby,' she said, clutching at the sleeve of the white dress. Lucynell looked straight at her and didn't seem to see her there at all. Mr. Shiftlet eased the car forward so that she had to move her hands.

The early afternoon was clear and open and surrounded by pale blue sky. Although the car would go only thirty miles an hour, Mr. Shiftlet imagined a terrific climb and dip and swerve that went entirely to his head so that he forgot his morning bitterness. He had always wanted an automobile but he had never been able to afford one before. He drove very fast because he wanted to make Mobile by nightfall.

Occasionally he stopped his thoughts long enough to look at Lucynell in the seat beside him. She had eaten the lunch as soon as they were out of the yard and now she was pulling the cherries off the hat one by one and throwing them out the window. He became depressed in spite of the car. He had driven about a hundred miles when he decided that she must be hungry again and at the next small town they came to, he stopped in front of an aluminium-painted eating place called The Hot Spot and took her in and ordered her a place of ham and grits. The ride had made her sleepy and as soon as she got up on the stool, she rested her head on the counter and shut her eyes. There was no-one in The Hot Spot but Mr. Shiftlet and the boy behind the counter, a pale youth with a greasy rag hung over his shoulder. Before he could dish up the food, she was snoring gently.

'Give it to her when she wakes up,' Mr. Shiftlet said. 'I'll pay for it now.'

The boy bent over her and stared at the long pink-gold hair and the half-shut sleeping eyes. Then he looked up and stared at Mr. Shiftlet. 'She looks like an angel of Gawd,' he murmured.

'Hitch-hiker,' Mr. Shiftlet explained. 'I can't wait. I got to make Tuscaloosa.'

The boy bent over again and very carefully touched his finger to a strand of the golden hair and Mr. Shiftlet left.

He was more depressed than ever as he drove on by himself. The late afternoon had grown hot and sultry and the country had flattened out. Deep in the sky a storm was preparing very slowly and without thunder as if it meant to drain every drop of air from the earth before it broke. There were times when Mr. Shiftlet preferred not to be alone. He felt too that a man with a car had a responsibility to others and he kept his eye out for a hitch-hiker. Occasionally he saw a sign that warned: 'Drive carefully. The life you save may be your own.'

The narrow road dropped off on either side into dry fields and here and there a shack or a filling station stood in a clearing. The sun began to set directly in front of the automobile. It was a reddening ball that through his windshield was slightly flat at the bottom and top. He saw a boy in overalls and a gray hat standing on the edge of the road and he slowed the car down and stopped in front of him. The boy didn't have his hand raised to thumb the ride, he was only standing there, but he had a small cardboard suitcase and his hat was set on his head in a way to indicate that he had left somewhere for good. 'Son,' Mr. Shiftlet said, 'I see you want a ride.'

The boy didn't say he did or didn't but he opened the door of the car and got in, and Mr. Shiftlet started driving again. The child held the suitcase on his lap and folded his arms on top of it. He turned his head and looked out the window away from Mr. Shiftlet. Mr. Shiftlet felt oppressed. 'Son,' he said after a minute, 'I got the best old mother in the world so I reckon you only got the second best.'

The boy gave him a quick dark glance and then turned his face back out the window.

'It's nothing so sweet,' Mr. Shiftlet continued, 'as a boy's mother. She taught him his first prayers at her knee, she give him love when no other would, she told him what was right and what wasn't, and she seen that he done the right thing. Son,' he said, 'I never rued a day in my life like the one I rued when I left that old mother of mine.'

The boy shifted in his seat but he didn't look at Mr. Shiftlet. He unfolded his arms and put one hand on the door handle.

'My mother was an angel of Gawd,' Mr. Shiftlet said in a very strained voice. 'He took her from heaven and giver to me and I left her.' His eyes were instantly clouded over with a mist of tears. The car was barely moving.

The boy turned angrily in the seat. 'You go to the devil!' he cried. 'My old woman is a flea bag and yours is a stinking pole cat!' and with that he flung the door open and jumped out with his suitcase into the ditch.

Mr. Shiftlet was so shocked that for about a hundred feet he drove along slowly with the door still open. A cloud, the exact color of the boy's hat and shaped like a turnip, had descended over the sun, and another, worse looking, crouched behind the car. Mr. Shiftlet felt that the rottenness of the world was about to engulf him. He raised his arm and let it fall again to his breast. 'Oh Lord!' he prayed. 'Break forth and wash the slime from this earth!'

The turnip continued slowly to descend. After a few minutes there was a guffawing peal of thunder from behind and fantastic raindrops, like tin-can tops, crashed over the rear of Mr. Shiftlet's car. Very quickly he stepped on the gas and with his stump sticking out the window he raced the galloping shower into Mobile.

GRAHAM GREENE

A Drive
In The Country

As every other night she listened to her father going round the house, locking the doors and windows. He was head clerk at Bergson's Export Agency, and lying in bed she would think with dislike that his home was like his office, run on the same lines, its safety preserved with the same meticulous care, so that he could present a faithful steward's account to the managing-director. Regularly every Sunday he presented the account, accompanied by his wife and two daughters, in the little neo-Gothic church in Park Road. They always had the same pew, they were always five minutes early, and her father sang loudly with no sense of tune, holding an outsize prayer book on the level of his eyes. 'Singing songs of exultation' – he was presenting the week's account (one household duly safeguarded) – 'marching to the Promised Land.' When they came out of church, she looked carefully away from the corner by the 'Bricklayers' Arms' where Fred always stood, a little lit because the Arms had been open for half an hour, with his air of unbalanced exultation.

She listened: the back door closed, she could hear the catch of the kitchen window click, and the restless pad of his feet going back to try the front door. It wasn't only the outside doors he locked: he locked the empty rooms, the bathroom, the lavatory. He was locking something out, but obviously it was something capable of penetrating his first defences. He raised his second line all the way up to bed.

She laid her ear against the thin wall of the jerry-built villa and could hear the faint voices from the neighbouring room; as she listened they came clearer as though she were turning the knob of a wireless set. Her mother said '... margarine in the cooking ...' and her father said '... much easier in fifteen years'. Then the bed creaked and there were dim sounds of tenderness and comfort between the two middle-aged strangers in the next room. In fifteen years, she thought unhappily, the house will be his; he had paid twenty-five pounds down and the rest he was paying month by month as rent. 'Of course,' he was in the habit of saying after a good meal, 'I've improved the property,' and he expected at least one of them to follow him into his study. 'I've wired this room for power,' he padded back past the little downstairs lavatory, 'this radiator', the final stroke of satisfaction, 'the garden', and if it was a fine evening he would fling the french window of the dining-room open on the little carpet of grass as carefully kept as a college lawn. 'A pile of bricks,' he'd say, 'that's all it was.' Five years of Saturday afternoons and fine Sundays had gone into the patch of turf, the surrounding flower-bed, the one apple-tree which regularly produced one crimson tasteless apple more each year.

'Yes,' he said, 'I've improved the property,' looking round for a nail to drive in , a weed to be uprooted. 'If we had to sell now, we should get back more than I've paid from the society.' It was more than a sense of property, it was a sense of honesty. Some people who bought their houses through the society let them go to rack and ruin and then cleared out.

She stood with her ear against the wall, a small, furious, immature figure. There was no more to be heard from the other room, but in her inner ear she still heard the chorus of a property owner, the tap-tap of a hammer, the scrape of a spade, the whistle of radiator steam, a key turning, a bolt pushed home, the little trivial sounds of men building barricades. She stood planning her treachery.

26

It was a quarter past ten; she had an hour in which to leave the house, but it did not take so long. There was really nothing to fear. They had played their usual rubber of three-handed bridge while her sister altered a dress for the local 'hop' next night; after the rubber she had boiled a kettle and brought in a pot of tea; then she had filled the hot-water bottles and put them in the beds while her father locked up. He had no idea whatever that she was an enemy.

She put on a scarf and a heavy coat because it was still cold at night; the spring was late that year, as her father commented, watching for the buds on the apple-tree. She didn't pack a suitcase; that would have reminded her too much of week-ends at the sea, a family expedition to Ostend from all of which one returned; she wanted to match the odd reckless quality of Fred's mind. This time she wasn't going to return. She went softly downstairs into the little crowded hall, unlocked the door. All was quiet upstairs, and she closed the door behind her.

She was touched by a faint feeling of guilt because she couldn't lock it from the outside. But her guilt vanished by the time she reached the end of the crazy-paved path and turned to the left down the road which after five years was still half made, past the gaps between the villas where the wounded fields remained grimly alive in the form of thin grass and heaps of clay and dandelions.

She walked fast, passing a long line of little garages like the graves in a Latin cemetery where the coffin lies below the fading photograph of its occupant. The cold night air touched her with exhilaration. She was ready for anything, as she turned by the Belisha beacon into the shuttered shopping street; she was like a recruit in the first months of a war. The choice made she could surrender her will to the strange, the exhilarating, the gigantic event.

Fred, as he had promised, was at the corner where the road turned down towards the church; she could taste the spirit on his lips as they kissed, and she was satisfied that no one else could have so adequately matched the occasion; his face was bright and reckless in the lamp-light, he was as exciting and strange to her as the adventure. He took her arm and ran her into a blind unlighted alley, then left her for a moment until two headlamps beamed softly at her out of the cavern. She cried with astonishment, 'You've got a car?' and felt the jerk of his nervous hand urging her towards it. 'Yes,' he said, 'do you like it?' grinding into second gear, changing clumsily into top as they came out between the shuttered windows.

She said, 'It's lovely. Let's drive a long way.'

'We will,' he said, watching the speedometer needle go quivering to fifty-five.

'Does it mean you've got a job?'

'There are no jobs,' he said, 'they don't exist any more than the Dodo. Did you see that bird?' he asked sharply, turning his headlights full on as they passed the turning to the housing estate and quite suddenly came out into the country between a café ('Draw in here'), a boot-shop ('Buy the shoes worn by your favourite film star'), and an undertaker's with a large white angel lit by a neon light.

'I didn't see any bird.'

'Not flying at the windscreen?'

'No.'

'I nearly hit it,' he said. 'It would have made a mess. Bad as those fellows who run someone down and don't stop. Should *we* stop? he asked, turning out his switchboard light so that they couldn't see the needle vibrate to sixty.

'Whatever you say,' she said, sitting deep in a reckless dream.

'You going to love me tonight?'

'Of course I am.'

'Never going back there?'

'No,' she said, abjuring the tap of hammer, the click of latch, the pad of slippered feet making the rounds.

'Want to know where we are going?'

'No.' A little flat cardboard copse ran forward into the green light and darkly by. A rabbit turned its scut and vanished into a hedge. He said, 'Have you any money?'

'Half a crown.'

'Do you love me?' For a long time she expended on his lips all she had patiently had to keep in reserve, looking the other way on Sunday mornings, saying nothing when his name came up at meals with disapproval. She expended herself against dry unresponsive lips as the car leapt ahead and his foot trod down on the accelerator. He said, 'It's the hell of a life.'

She echoed him, 'The hell of a life.'

He said, 'There's a bottle in my pocket. Have a drink.'

'I don't want one.

'Give me one then. It has a screw top,' and with one hand on her and one on the wheel he tipped his head, so that she could pour a little whisky into his mouth out of the quarter bottle. 'Do you mind?' he said.

'Of course I don't mind.'

'You can't save,' he said, 'on ten shillings a week pocket-money. I lay it out the best I can. It needs a hell of a lot of thought. To give variety. Half a crown on Weights. Three and six on whisky. A shilling on the pictures. That leaves three shillings for beer. I take my fun once a week and get it over.'

The whisky had dribbled on to his tie and the smell filled the small coupé. It pleased her. It was *his* smell. He said, 'They grudge it me. They think I ought to get a job. When you're that age you don't realize there aren't any jobs for some of us—any more for ever.'

'I know,' she said. 'They are old.'

'How's your sister?' he asked abruptly; the bright glare swept the road ahead of them clean of small scurrying birds and animals.

'She's going to the hop tomorrow. I wonder where we shall be...'

He wouldn't be drawn; he had his own idea and kept it to himself.

'I'm loving this.'

He said, 'There's a club out this way. At a road-house. Mick made me a member. Do you know Mick?'

'No.'

'Mick's all right. If they know you, they'll serve you drinks till midnight. We'll look in there. Say hullo to Mick. And then in the morning—we'll decide that later when we've had a few drinks.'

'Have you the money?' A small village, fast asleep already behind closed doors and windows, sailed down the hill towards them as if it was being carried smoothly by a landslide into the scarred plain from which they'd come. A low grey Norman church, an inn without a sign, a clock striking eleven. He said, 'Look in the back. There's a suitcase there.'

'It's locked.'

'I forgot the key,' he said.

'What's in it?'

'A few things,' he said vaguely. 'We could pop them for drinks.'

'What about a bed?'

'There's the car. You are not scared, are you?'

'No,' she said. 'I'm not scared. This is—' but she hadn't words for the damp cold wind, the darkness, the strangeness, the smell of whisky and the rushing car. 'It moves,' she said. 'We must have gone a long way already. This is real country,' seeing an owl sweep low on furry wings over a ploughed field.

'You've got to go farther than this for real country,' he said. 'You won't find it yet on *this* road. We'll be at the road-house soon.'

She discovered in herself a nostalgia for their dark windy solitary progress. She said, 'Need we go to the club? Can't we go farther into the country?'

He looked sideways at her; he had always been open to *any* suggestion: like some meteorological instrument, he was made for the winds to blow through. 'Of course,' he said, 'anything you like.' He didn't give the club a second thought; they swept past it a moment later, a long lit Tudor bungalow, a crash of voices, a bathing-pool filled for some reason with hay. It was immediately behind them, a patch of light whipping round a corner out of sight.

He said, 'I suppose this is country now. They none of them got farther than the club. We're quite alone now. We could lie in these fields till doomsday as far as *they* are concerned, though I suppose a ploughman...if they do plough here.' He raised his foot from the accelerator and let the car's speed gradually diminish. Somebody had left a wooden gate open into a field and he turned the car in; they jolted a long way down the field beside the hedge and came to a standstill. He turned off the headlamps and they sat in the tiny glow of the switchboard light. 'Peaceful,' he said uneasily; and they heard a screech owl hunting overhead and a small rustle in the hedge where something went into hiding. They belonged to the city; they hadn't a name for anything round them; the tiny buds breaking in the bushes were nameless. He nodded at a group of dark trees at the hedge ends. 'Oaks?'

'Elms?' she asked, and their mouths went together in a mutual ignorance. The touch excited her; she was ready for the most reckless act; but from his mouth, the dry spiritous lips, she gained a sense that he was less excited than he had hoped to be.

She said, to reassure herself, 'It's good to be here – miles away from anyone we know.'

'I dare say Mick's there. Down the road.'

'Does he know?'

'Nobody knows.'

She said, 'That's how I wanted it. How did you get this car?'

He grinned at her with unbalanced amusement. 'I saved from the ten shillings.'

'No but how? Did someone lend it you?'

'Yes,' he said. He suddenly pushed the door open and said. 'Let's take a walk.'

'We've never walked in the country before.' She took his arm, and she could feel the tense nerves responding to her touch. It was what she liked; she couldn't tell what he would do next. She said, 'My father calls you crazy. I like you crazy. What's all this stuff?' kicking at the ground.

'Clover,' he said, 'isn't it? I don't know.' It was like being in a foreign city where you can't understand the names on shops, the traffic signs: nothing to catch hold of, to hold you down to this and that, adrift together in a dark vacuum. 'Shouldn't you turn on the headlamps?' she said. 'It won't be so easy finding our way back. There's not much moon.' Already they seemed to have gone a long way from the car; she couldn't see it clearly any longer.

'We'll find our way,' he said. 'Somehow. Don't worry.' At the hedge end they came to the trees. He pulled a twig down and felt the sticky buds. 'What is it? Beech?'

'I don't know.'

He said, 'If it had been warmer, we could have slept out here. You'd think we might have had that much luck, tonight

31

of all nights. But it's cold and it's going to rain.'

'Let's come in the summer,' but he didn't answer. Some other wind had blown, she could tell it, and already he had lost interest in her. There was something hard in his pocket; it hurt her side; she put her hand in. The metal chamber had absorbed all the cold there had been in the windy ride. She whispered fearfully, 'Why are you carrying that?' She had always before drawn a line round his recklessness. When her father had said he was crazy she had secretly and possessively smiled because she thought she knew the extent of his craziness. Now, while she waited for him to answer her, she could feel his craziness go on and on, out of her reach, out of her sight; she couldn't see where it ended; it had no end, she couldn't possess it any more than she could possess a darkness or a desert.

'Don't be scared,' he said. 'I didn't mean you to find that tonight.' He suddenly became more tender than he had ever been; he put his hand on her breast; it came from his fingers, a great soft meaningless flood of tenderness. He said, 'Don't you see? Life's hell. There's nothing we can do.' He spoke very gently, but she had never been more aware of his recklessness: he was open to every wind, but the wind now seemed to have set from the east: it blew like sleet through his words. 'I haven't a penny,' he said. 'We can't live on nothing. It's no good hoping that I'll get a job.' He repeated, 'There aren't any more jobs any more. And every year, you know, there's less chance, because there are more people younger than I am.'

'But why,' she said, 'have we come—?'

He became softly and tenderly lucid. 'We do love each other, don't we? We can't live without each other. It's no good hanging around, is it, waiting for our luck to change. We don't even get a fine night,' he said, feeling for rain with his hand. 'We can have a good time tonight—in the car—and then in the morning— '

'No, no,' she said. She tried to get away from him. 'I couldn't. It's horrible. I never said— '

'You wouldn't know anything,' he said gently and inexorably. Her words, she could realize now, had never made any real impression; he was swayed by them but no more than he was swayed by anything: now that the wind had set, it was

32

like throwing scraps of paper towards the sky to speak at all, or to argue. He said, 'Of course we neither of us believe in God, but there may be a chance, and it's company, going together like that.' He added with pleasure, 'It's a gamble,' and she remembered more occasions than she could count when their last coppers had gone ringing down in fruit machines.

He pulled her closer and said with complete assurance, 'We love each other. It's the only way, you know. You can trust me.' He was like a skilled logician; he knew all the stages of the argument. She despaired of catching him out on any point but the premise: we love each other. *That* she doubted for the first time, faced by the mercilessness of his egotism. He repeated, 'It will be company.'

She said, 'There must be some way ...'

'Why *must*?'

'Otherwise, people would be doing it all the time— everywhere!'

'They are,' he said triumphantly, as if it were more important for him to find his argument flawless than to find—well, a way, a way to go on living. 'You've only got to read the newspapers,' he said. He whispered gently, endearingly, as if he thought the very sound of the words tender enought to dispel all fear. 'They call it a suicide pact. It's happening all the time.'

'I couldn't. I haven't the nerve.'

'You needn't do anything,' he said. 'I'll do it all.'

His calmness horrified her. 'You mean—you'd kill me?'

He said, 'I love you enough for that, I promise it won't hurt you.' He might have been persuading her to play some trivial and uncongenial game. 'We shall be together always.' He added rationally, 'Of course, if there *is* an always,' and suddenly she saw his love as a mere flicker of gas flame playing on the marshy depth of his irresponsibility, but now she realized that it was without any limit at all; it closed over the head. She pleaded, 'There are things we can sell. That suitcase.'

She knew that he was watching her with amusement, that he had rehearsed all her arguments and had an answer; he was only pretending to take her seriously. 'We might get fifteen shillings,' he said. 'We could live a day on that—but we shouldn't have much fun.'

'The things inside it?'

'Ah, that's another gamble. They might be worth thirty shillings. Three days, that would give us—with economy.'

'We might get a job.'

'I've been trying for a good many years now.'

'Isn't there the dole?'

'I'm not an insured worker. I'm one of the ruling class.'

'Your people, they'd give us something.'

'But we've got our pride, haven't we?' he said with remorseless conceit.

'The man who lent you the car?'

He said, 'You remember Cortez, the fellow who burnt his boats? I've burned mine. I've *got* to kill myself. You see, I stole that car. We'd be stopped in the next town. It's too late even to go back.' He laughed; he had reached the climax of his argument and there was nothing more to dispute about. She could tell that he was perfectly satisfied and perfectly happy. It infuriated her. '*You've* got to, maybe. But I haven't. Why should I kill myself? What right have you—?' She dragged herself away from him and felt against her back the rough massive trunk of the living tree.

'Oh,' he said in an irritated tone, 'of course if you like to go on without me.' She had admired his conceit; he had always carried his unemployment with a manner. Now you could no longer call it conceit: it was a complete lack of any values. 'You can go home,' he said, 'though I don't quite know how – I can't drive back because I'm staying here. You'll be able to go to the hop tomorrow night. And there's a whist-drive, isn't there in the church hall? My dear, I wish you joy of home.'

There was a savagery in his manner. He took security, peace, order in his teeth and worried them so that she couldn't help feeling a little pity for what they had joined in despising: a hammer tapped at her heart, driving in a nail here and there. She tried to think of a bitter retort, for after all there was something to be said for the negative virtues of doing no injury, of simply going on, as her father was going on for another fifteen years. But the next moment she felt no anger. They had trapped each other. He had always wanted this: the dark field, the

weapon in his pocket, the escape and the gamble; but she less
honestly had wanted a little of both worlds: irresponsibility
and a safe love, danger and a secure heart.

He said, 'I'm going now. Are you coming?'

'No,' she said. He hesitated; the recklessness for a moment
wavered; a sense of something lost and bewildered came to
her through the dark. She wanted to say: Don't be a fool. Leave
the car where it is. Walk back with me, and we'll get a lift
home, but she knew any thought of hers had occurred to him
and been answered already. Ten shillings a week, no job, getting older. Endurance was a virtue of one's fathers.

He suddenly began to walk fast down the hedge; he
couldn't see where he was going; he stumbled on a root and
she heard him swear. 'Damnation'—the little commonplace
sound in the darkness overwhelmed her with pain and
horror. She cried out, 'Fred. Fred. Don't do it,' and began to
run in the opposite direction. She couldn't stop him and she
wanted to be out of hearing. A twig broke under her foot like
a shot, and the owl screamed across the ploughed field
beyond the hedge. It was like a rehearsal with sound effects.
But when the real shot came, it was quite different: a thud like
a gloved hand striking a door and no cry at all. She didn't
notice it at first and afterwards she thought that she had never
been conscious of the exact moment when her lover ceased to
exist.

She bruised herself against the car, running blindly; a blue-
spotted Woolworth handkerchief lay on the seat in the light of
the switchboard bulb. She nearly took it, but no, she thought,
no one must know that I have been here. She turned out the
light and picked her way as quietly as she could across the
clover. She could begin to be sorry when she was safe. She
wanted to close a door behind her, thrust a bolt down, hear
the catch grip.

It wasn't ten minutes walk down the deserted lane to the
road-house. Tipsy voices spoke a foreign language, though it
was the language Fred had spoken. She could hear the clink of
coins in fruit machines, the hiss of soda; she listened to these
sounds like an enemy, planning her escape. They frightened
her like something mindless: there was no appeal one could

make to that egotism. It was simply a Want to be satisfied; it gaped at her like a mouth. A man was trying to wind up his car; the self-starter wouldn't work. He said, 'I'm a Bolshie. Of course I'm a Bolshie. I believe—'

A thin girl with red hair sat on the step and watched him. 'You're all wrong,' she said.

'I'm a Liberal Conservative.'

'You *can't* be a liberal Conservative.'

'Do you love me?'

'I love Joe.'

'You *can't* love Joe.'

'Let's go home, Mike.'

The man tried to wind up the car again, and she came up to them as if she'd come out of the club and said, 'Give me a lift?'

'Course. Delighted. Get in.'

'Won't the car go?'

'No.'

'Have you flooded—?'

'That's an idea.' He lifted the bonnet and she pressed the self-starter. It began to rain slowly and heavily and drenchingly, the kind of rain you always expect to fall on graves, and her thoughts went down the lane towards the field, the hedge, the trees—oak, beech, elm? She imagined the rain on his face, the pool collecting in each eye-socket and streaming down on either side the nose. But she could feel nothing but gladness because she had escaped from him.

'Where are you going?' she said.

'Devizes.'

'I thought you might be going to London.'

'Where do you want to go?'

'Golding's Park.'

'Let's go to Golding's Park.'

The red-haired girl said, 'I am going in, Mike. It's raining.'

'Aren't you coming?'

'I'm going to find Joe.'

'All right.' He smashed his way out of the little car-park, bending his mudguard on a wooden post, scraping the paint of another car.

'That's the wrong way,' she said.

'We'll turn.' He backed the car into a ditch and out again. 'Was a good party,' he said. The rain came down harder; it blinded the windscreen and the electric wipe wouldn't work, but her companion didn't care. He drove straight on at forty miles an hour; it was an old car, it wouldn't do any more; the rain leaked through the hood. He said, 'Twis' that knob. Have a tune,' and when she turned it and the dance music came through, he said, 'That's Harry Roy. Know him anywhere,' driving into the thick wet night carrying the hot music with them. Presently he said, 'A friend of mine, one of the best, you'd know him, Peter Weatherall. You know him.'

'No.'

'You must know Peter. Haven't seen him about lately. Goes off on the drink for weeks. They sent out an SOS for Peter once in the middle of the dance music. 'Missing from Home'. We were in the car. We had a laugh about that.'

She said, 'Is that what people do—when people are missing?'

'Know this tune,' he said. 'This isn't Harry Roy. This is Alf Cohen.'

She said suddenly, 'You're Mike, aren't you? Wouldn't *you* lend—'

He sobered up. 'Stony broke,' he said. 'Comrades in misfortune. Try Peter. Why do you want to go to Golding's Park?'

'My home.'

'You mean you live there?'

'Yes.' She said, 'Be careful. There's a speed limit here.' He was perfectly obedient. He raised his foot and let the car crawl at fifteen miles an hour. The lamp standards marched unsteadily to meet them and lit his face: he was quite old, forty if a day, ten years older than Fred. He wore a striped tie and she could see his sleeve was frayed. He had more than ten shillings a week, but perhaps not so very much more. His hair was going thin.

'You can drop me here,' she said. He stopped the car and she got out and the rain went on. He followed her on to the road. 'Let me come in?' he asked. She shook her head; the rain wetted them through; behind her was the pillar-box, the Belisha beacon, the road through the housing estate. 'Hell of a life,' he said politely, holding her hand, while the rain drummed on the hood of the cheap car and ran down his face, across his collar and the school tie. But she felt no pity, no attraction, only a faint horror and repulsion. A kind of dim recklessness gleamed in his wet eye, as the hot music of Alf Cohen's band streamed from the car, a faded irresponsibility. 'Le's go back,' he said, 'le's go somewhere. Le's go for a ride in the country. Le's go to Maidenhead,' holding her hand limply.

She pulled it away, he didn't resist, and walked down the half-made road to No. 64. The crazy paving in the front garden seemed to hold her feet firmly up. She opened the door and heard through the dark and the rain a car grind into second gear and drone away—certainly not towards Maidenhead or Devizes or the country. Another wind must have blown.

Her father called down from the first landing: 'Who's there?'

'It's me,' she said. She explained, 'I had a feeling you'd left the door unbolted.'

'And had I?'

'No,' she said gently, 'it's bolted all right,' driving the bolt softly and firmly home. She waited till his door closed. She touched the radiator to warm her fingers—he had put it in himself, he had improved the property; in fifteen years, she thought, it will be ours. She was quite free from pain, listening to the rain on the roof; he had been over the whole roof that winter inch by inch, there was nowhere for the rain to enter. It was kept outside, drumming on the shabby hood, pitting the clover field. She stood by the door, feeling only the faint repulsion she always had for things weak and crippled, thinking, 'It isn't tragic at all,' and looking down with an emotion like tenderness at the flimsy bolt from a sixpenny store any man could have broken, but which a Man had put in, the head clerk of Bergson's.

GEOFFREY DEAN

Talks With My Uncle Moro

Uncle Moro was not really my uncle at all… He was an intiner-ant farm worker who arrived at 'Pandora' each year around harvest time and stayed through the summer. Uncle Moro was, we guessed, about sixty years old; but it was hard to tell and Uncle Moro never offered his age to anyone. If ever pressed he would just smile and shrug his shoulders, and if he did say anything it was invariably something enigmatic, like, he was as old as he seemed to be.

We called him Uncle Moro because we thought of him as part of the family. Nobody could remember exactly how many years it was he had been coming to the farm for harvest time, but it was as long as I could remember.

He wasn't a foreigner, as his name may suggest; he was in fact more Australian than anybody I knew. In many ways a left-over from the Henry Lawson era, a man who was fitted more for the back-blocks and the bush rather than the city and suburbs.

Nobody knew very much about him – where he lived, or where he spent the time when he wasn't at 'Pandora'. I imagined he tramped the roads from place to place the whole length of the continent in search of seasonal work. Some of the locals, less kindly, suggested he was a reformed alcoholic, because he always refused a glass of beer. Others, more imaginative, reckoned from the way that he talked he was more likely a professional man who was running away from something, be it the law, or family disgrace. Whatever, it remained Uncle Moro's secret.

Sometimes he would let out bits of information about his past, but usually said in such a way you couldn't ever be sure if it was true or not. For instance, he was inclined to tell people that Moro was the name the Aboriginals called him. But I knew this wasn't strictly true. He told me once he only said things like that to satisfy other people's insatiable curiosity.

'It's a sad thing,' he told me, 'but people are never happy until they got you categorised. If you let them they'll put you in a little box with all your details on the lid – just like some species of moth. In fact, I've always been called Moro, ever since I was a child – I forget why.' He smiled, 'The Aboriginals did call me Moro because it was my name.'

The Aboriginals seemed of special interest to him.

'Why did you leave them?' I asked him once when we were hoeing a paddock of potatoes.

He thought about it for a while, 'Well, firstly I suppose, it was because I had a tribal marriage to one of their girls and she died. But it wasn't only that ... I couldn't have stayed forever because their culture was too strong. You know, in spite of what most people think our Aboriginal race has an intricate culture and a spiritualism of considerable sophistication ...'

He sighed, as if remembering some past sadness. 'Those poor drunken wrecks who are sometimes seen existing on the fringes of our cities are outside their natural environment ... they are only the expression of their sorrow because they are unable to view life the way we do. I suppose I left them because it was the same with me ... only in reverse. In spite of my youth I could never keep up to Uncle Moro when it came to hoeing the cash crops. Invariably he'd slow down to suit my speed, or he'd wait at the end of each row in the shade of a tree and suck his pipe until I caught up to him. If I ever expressed frustration at my inability to match him he'd simply smile knowingly.

'It's a matter of rhythm,' he'd say, 'and rhythm is a state of intuition that has little to do with the ordinary things … like strength.'

Peeved, I'd asked him what he meant.

He thought for a while before he answered.

'Have you ever heard the story about the centipede?' he asked. I shook my head.

'Well the story goes that one day a toad stopped a centipede and asked him how it was the centipede managed to walk so well, seeing he had a hundred legs to control. The centipede sat down and thought about it for a long time – nobody had ever put the question to him before. 'You perplex me,' he told the toad, 'I just do it. Perhaps it has something to do with co-ordination of brain and muscle? Or then, perhaps it is due to the fact that I have a highly developed nervous system? I'm afraid I don't know for sure.'

'Still pondering the problem, the centipede decided to move off, and the curious thing was that somehow he had lost his rhythm. That poor centipede was never the same again … he spent the remainder of his life tripping over one or other of his many legs and struggling out of ditches he had fallen into.'

'But why?' I asked.

Uncle Moro grinned. 'Because, I suppose, he had failed to reconcile rationality with intuitive knowledge.'

I nodded, but I still wasn't sure what Uncle Moro meant.

Uncle Moro picked up his hoe and set into the next row. I followed him, trying to keep up.

He stopped for a moment and watched me. 'For a start,' he said, 'you could try to be more relaxed.'

I grinned a little ashamedly and slowed down, and the curious thing was, at the end of the row I had almost caught up to him.

My father said Uncle Moro was not only a thinker, but the best workman he'd ever had at 'Pandora', and that he'd like him to stay with us all the year.

But Uncle Moro told him if he stayed the whole year he might not be such a good worker. 'I might become bored with doing the same things all the year … year in, year out. And when you're bored you work less and daydream more.'

Sometimes I didn't understand what Uncle Moro meant at all, but it didn't seem to matter, for I often remembered things he had said years later and they made sense then.

'Most people only work to make money to buy food to give them strength to make more money,' Uncle Moro told me another time. 'It wasn't meant to be like that. And in spite of what many people seem to think it hasn't improved since I was a boy...quite the reverse. When your father gets a machine to weed the potatoes, you'll understand what I mean.'

One February my little sister got an earache which wouldn't get better, and two weeks later she awoke in the middle of the night screaming. Then she began to fit. She was rushed off to the hospital in a coma and for the following week or so there was doubt whether she would recover. The district churches arranged special services to pray for her and I prayed too. I had never done that before. In those occasional times I had been to church previously I had only mouthed the words, at best half-formed, miming in rhythm with the others. They seemed to know how but I didn't. But when I did pray for my sister I was surprised how easily it came.

I asked Uncle Moro later whether he believed in God. We were stacking hay into the barn for winter feeding. Now recovered completely, my sister was due home that evening.

With a bale balanced in his arms Uncle Moro shrugged as he answered. 'Emily got well didn't she? Why don't you just accept that?'

'It could have nothing to do with the prayers,' I said. 'She might have got well anyway.'

'She might,' he said. 'But the way it was it let everyone feel they were contributing — even yourself, hey?'

'Yes,' I said , 'it did.'

'So, why worry?' Uncle Moro smiled suddenly. 'Can't you see it doesn't matter. It's a mystery – unsolved, and perhaps that's the very reason it seemed to work.'

I still didn't understand what he meant and I told him so.

He stopped work again, his face thoughtful, recalling old memories.

'Well,' he said finally, 'praying can be more complicated

than it sometimes seems. Once I worked on a farm in a district where they'd had a continuing and crippling drought for nearly a year. A group of local farmers decided to arrange for a special church service to pray for rain. Well, they prayed themselves hoarse, and, do you know, just three days later there was a great storm. As you could guess, most of the farmers were jubilant, but others, those caught unawares, suffered heavy stock and crop losses. Half the town's people were flooded out of their homes and a local ploughing contractor went broke because the flood waters washed his tractor into the river and smashed it to pieces. There was a lot of resentment in that town for a long time after.'

He paused a moment as he threw up another bale of hay. He turned towards me, giving me another brief smile. 'So you see,' he said, 'it's not the prayin' that's important — only the result.'

I never did find out whether Uncle Moro believed in God or not...

Uncle Moro didn't seem to own much. 'Possessions tie you down...there's more sleep lost worrying about your possessions than there is worrying about loved ones ... and in the end nothing really belongs to anyone.' I heard him say it more than once.

He didn't even have a car to get around in like the other workers. He always arrived at the farm on foot or in Jack Burgess' hire car. He left the same way.

The only clothes he had were two pairs of dark green work trousers and two khaki shirts without collars. He also had a couple of sets of long-johns, which he wore under his clothes even on the the hottest days. Although he sometimes took off his shirt, I never saw him without the top of his long-johns on.

He also had a bluey-coat[1] which he wore when the weather was colder. Hanging on the peg in the porch, it always seemed to smell of damp earth and stale milk.

When he went to town, which was seldom, he changed into an old navy blue pinstriped suit, which looked too small for him. Underneath the suit he wore his spare clean khaki shirt.

Once, out of curiosity, I stole a look into the old haversack he carried his clothes and personal possessions in. Other than his clothes, all that was in there was his shaving gear, his spare pipe and tobacco, a mouth organ, a couple of letters that were very crumpled and discoloured and a small framed picture of a young woman with huge eyes, long dark hair and a thin sad face. Because I had stolen a look in his bag, I never could ask him about the picture…

Sometimes, when it was a warm evening and the gnats and moths weren't too bad, we'd all sit out on the dry summer lawn and drink cold juice from the refrigerator and listen to Uncle Moro play his mouth organ. Most of the tunes he played were unfamiliar, but there was so much feeling there it didn't seem to matter. My mother also used to play the violin a bit, and everyone used to try to get her and Uncle Moro to play together, but he never would.

'I'm self-taught and I've been playing by myself so long now I find it too difficult to play with anyone else.'

If pushed further he'd just smile and say he had to go to bed, because at his age he needed plenty of sleep. But his light usually remained on later than anyone's. My mother suggested he may be reading, but I didn't think so, he never had any books of his own and I never saw him borrow a book from our bookcase or even a newspaper from the table…

Once a month, after each pay day, Uncle Moro used to walk to town, 'to buy a few little things for myself,' he said. But more often than not he bought presents for us and only a bit of tobacco or toothpaste for himself.

The townspeople considered Uncle Moro a bit of a joke in his ancient blue suit and heavy boots. They used to talk to him as if he were simple. They were inclined to raise their voices and speak slowly and carefully, as if he were incapable of understanding the language. Uncle Moro didn't seem to notice, but I did. Because of it, I used to get annoyed with them and stand there sullenly glaring while they served him.

But I was wrong, he did notice, and on one such-occasion he told me I should not be so judgmental. 'They are people whose experience is limited, they are only trying to be helpful in their own way.'

'They laugh behind your back,' I told him angrily. 'That's not being helpful.' He only shrugged. 'It's better than throwin' stones. Perhaps they only laugh because they are embarrassed and don't know what to say.'

It was the first time I felt anger towards him. 'You are so tolerant, I sometimes wonder whether you care.'

He looked at me with some surprise. He didn't deny it, he just asked me a question instead. 'How old are you, boy?'

'Fourteen,' I told him. But the resentment remained. 'Though I don't know why I should tell you my age, when you don't tell anyone yours.'

We were sitting on a wooden bench in a small corner block that once had been a butcher's shop, until it got burned down. The local council had put down a small lawn and seat, because it had been an eyesore and it didn't seem the butcher was ever going to find the money to rebuild his shop.

Uncle Moro smiled and nodded, 'I was seventy-six last birthday, and the reason I don't tell anyone is I don't want to be treated as an old man.'

I found it hard to believe. I thought he may have been joking with me. 'But, everyone thinks you're only about sixty.' I said.

He thought about it as he sucked at his pipe. 'Do they indeed? Well, well … then sixty I'll be.' He looked at me closely for a second. 'But what about you? About eighteen maybe? How does that sound?'

I recovered my good humour and nodded and together we walked back to the shops where, as usual, Uncle Moro bought a small present for everyone and only some tobacco and razor blades for himself.

While I was waiting for him I saw a book on one of the shelves. I flicked through the pages and decided to buy it. Later, going home in the taxi, I gave it to him.

'What's this?' he asked.

I was embarrassed. 'It's a present … for you. You always buy everyone presents and nobody buys you one. I thought you'd like it.'

He turned the small volume in his hands. It seemed almost too delicate for him to handle. He was looking out the window when he spoke. 'I don't have my glasses with me ... what's it called and who wrote it?' 'It's called, *Great Philosophers*,' I told him. 'Lots of people wrote in it. One of them...a man called Bertrand Russell, writes a bit like you talk.' He was still staring out the window. At what I don't know. We were passing Herb Mathews' dairy at the time and there was nothing much to look at there.

I heard Uncle Moro sigh when he finally answered. 'Is that so ... Russell, ay? Well, well.' He tucked the book gently into his inside pocket and just stared to the front all the way home...

As usual, Uncle Moro left 'Pandora' at the beginning of autumn. He shook hands with my father at the gate.

'Are you sure you don't want me to drive you to town?' My father asked.

Uncle Moro looked along the road and then up at the clear blue sky. 'No thanks – on such a day I'll enjoy the walk.'

My mother kissed him lightly on the cheek. I wish you'd stay.'

Uncle Moro smiled. 'You'd get sick of me under your feet all day, Mary.'

He picked up my sister and gave her a hug. She squealed with delight. Then he took my hand in both of his. 'And you work hard at school,' he told me. 'And never stop thinking — there, or ever. Okay?' We watched him stride off down the lane, his old haversack slung casually over one shoulder of the blue pin-striped suit. With the sun slanting down on him like that — shading out the details – the dark retreating figure could have been any age, so positive was his gait...

Uncle Moro didn't get back the following spring. A letter arrived late in November, explaining why he couldn't come. According to the letter Uncle Moro was in a nursing home. The matron explained that Uncle Moro had asked her to write on his behalf – to say he was sorry he couldn't be there for the harvest, but he hoped to be back again the following year.

But later we got a phone message from the home saying Uncle Moro had taken a turn for the worse. My father and mother decided we should all take a trip to the city to visit him.

We got there in the late morning and went to the room number marked on the letter, but the room was empty. I knew it was Uncle Moro's room though, because I recognised the book I had given him and the picture of the young woman with the long hair on the bedside table. I picked up the book and flicked through the pages. The room smelled of soap and disinfectant.

My father was just about to go and find him when the matron arrived. She looked at us with some surprise. 'You must be the people I wrote to. I'm sorry, I tried to ring you a second time ... he went so quickly ... there seemed no way I could let you know in time. Are you family?' My father nodded dumbly. 'Eh, yes ... he was an uncle.'

The matron began to absently fuss with the perfectly made bed. 'Such a lovely man,' she said. 'So well-mannered and polite ... and intelligent. Everyone here loved him – he didn't want me to contact anyone at first. He didn't want anyone to worry. I finally squeezed your name out of him and wrote myself ... so sad ... everyone should have someone at the end.'

Outside the sun was shining. A day not unlike the day earlier in the year when Uncle Moro strode off so confidently to town.

'I'll have to arrange the funeral,' my father said. He went off towards the office and the rest of us sat in the rose garden and waited.

My sister began sobbing and my mother put an arm around her. With her free hand she waved her handkerchief in the general direction of Uncle Moro's room. She seemed almost resentful.

'If only he could have written earlier ... we could have been here ... he should have let us know.'

I remembered Uncle Moro and me sitting on another bench, towards the end of the summer before. I remembered how he had confessed his true age and asked me to keep it a secret. I thought about the book I had given him, and driving home in Jack Burgess' car. The one he couldn't read the title of, because he didn't have his glasses with him. The book that now lay on his bedside table, unopened and new as the day I had given it to him. I began to realise there was another secret of Uncle Moro's I had to keep.

1 A 'bluey-coat' is a heavy, woollen, three-quarter-length coat, always navy blue, worn by fishermen, bushmen, miners, etc.

A *Father*

One Wednesday morning in mid-May Mr Bhowmick woke up as he usually did at 5:43 a.m., checked his Rolex against the alarm clock's digital readout, punched down the alarm (set for 5:45), then nudged his wife awake. She worked as a claims investigator for an insurance company that had an office in a nearby shopping mall. She didn't really have to leave the house until 8:30, but she liked to get up early and cook him a big breakfast. Mr Bhowmick had to drive a long way to work. He was a naturally dutiful, cautious man, and he set the alarm clock early enough to accommodate a margin for accidents.

While his wife, in a pink nylon negligee she had paid for with her own MasterCard card, made him a new version of French toast from a clipping ('Eggs-cellent Recipes!') Scotch-taped to the inside of a kitchen cupboard, Mr Bhowmick brushed his teeth. He brushed, he gurgled with the loud, hawking noises that he and his brother had been taught as children to make in order to flush clean not merely teeth but also tongue and palate.

After that he showered, then, back in the bedroom again, he recited prayers in Sanskrit to Kali, the patron goddess of his family, the goddess of wrath and vengeance. In the pokey flat

49

of his childhood in Ranchi, Bihar, his mother had given over a whole bedroom to her collection of gods and goddesses. Mr Bhowmick couldn't be that extravagant in Detroit. His daughter, twenty-six and an electrical engineer, slept in the other of the two bedrooms in his apartment. But he had done his best. He had taken Woodworking I and II at a nearby recreation center and built a grotto for the goddess. Kali-Mata was eight inches tall, made of metal and painted a glistening black so that the metal glowed like the oiled, black skin of a peasant woman. And though Kali-Mata was totally nude except for a tiny gilt crown and a garland strung together from sinners' chopped off heads, she looked warm, cozy, *pleased*, in her makeshift wooden shrine in Detroit. Mr Bhowmick had gathered quite a crowd of admiring, fellow woodworkers in those final weeks of decoration.

'Hurry it up with the prayers,' his wife shouted from the kitchen. She was an agnostic, a believer in ambition, not grace. She frequently complained that his prayers had gotten so long that soon he wouldn't have time to go to work, play duplicate bridge with the Ghosals, or play the tabla in the Bengali Association's one Sunday per month musical soirees. Lately she'd begun to drain him in a wholly new way. He wasn't praying, she nagged; he was shutting her out of his life. There'd be no peace in the house until she hid Kali-Mata in a suitcase.

She nagged, and he threatened to beat her with his shoe as his father had threatened his mother: it was the thrust and volley of marriage. There was no question of actually taking off a shoe and applying it to his wife's body. She was bigger than he was. And, secretly , he admired her for having the nerve, the agnosticism, which as a college boy in backward Bihar he too had claimed.

'I have time,' he shot at her. He was still wrapped in a damp terry towel.

'You have time for everything but domestic life.'

It was the fault of the shopping mall that his wife had started to buy pop psychology paperbacks. These paperbacks preached that for couples who could sit down and talk about their 'relationship,' life would be sweet again. His engineer

daughter was on his wife's side. She accused him of holding
things in.

'Face it, Dad,' she said. 'You have an affect deficit.'

But surely everyone had feelings they didn't want to talk
about or talk over. He definitely did not want to blurt out anything about the sick-in-the-guts sensations that came over him
most mornings and that he couldn't bubble down with Alka-
Seltzer or smother with Gas-X. The women in his family were
smarter than him. They were cheerful, outgoing, more American somehow.

How could he tell these bright, mocking women that in the
5:43 a.m. darkness, he sensed invisible presences: gods and
snakes frolicked in the master bedroom, little white sparks of
cosmic static crackled up the legs of his pajamas. Something
was out there in the dark, something that could invent accidents and coincidences to remind mortals that even in Detroit
they were no more than mortal. His wife would label this
paranoia and dismiss it. Paranoia, premonition: whatever it
was, it had begun to undermine his composure.

Take this morning. Mr Bhowmick had woken up from a pleasant dream about a man taking a Club Med vacation, and the
postdream satisfaction has lasted through the shower, but when
he'd come back to the shrine in the bedroom, he'd noticed all at
once how scarlet and saucy was the tongue that Kali-Mata stuck
out at the world. Surely he had not lavished such alarming
detail, such admonitory colors on that flap of flesh.

Watch out, ambulatory sinners. Be careful out there, the
goddess warned him, and not with the affection of Sergeant
Esterhaus, either.

'French toast must be eaten hot-hot,' his wife nagged.
'Otherwise they'll taste like rubber.'

Mr Bhowmick laid the trousers of a two-trouser suit he had
bought on sale that winter against his favorite tweed jacket.
The navy stripes in the trousers and the small, navy tweed
flecks in the jacket looked quite good together. So what if
the Chief Engineer had already started wearing summer
cottons?

'I am coming, I am coming,' he shouted back. 'You want me

to eat hot-hot, you start the frying only when I am sitting down. You didn't learn anything from Mother in Ranchi?'

'Mother cooked French toast from fancy recipes? I mean French Sandwich Toast with complicated filling?'

He came into the room to give her his testiest look. 'You don't know the meaning of complicated cookery. And Mother had to get the coal fire of the *chula* going first.'

His daughter was already at the table. 'Why don't you break down and buy her a microwave oven? That's what I mean about sitting down and talking things out.' She had finished her orange juice. She took a plastic measure of Slim-Fast out of its can and poured the powder into a glass of skim milk. 'It's ridiculous.'

Babli was not the child he would have chosen as his only heir. She was brighter certainly than the sons and daughters of the other Bengalis he knew in Detroit, and she had been the only female student in most of her classes at Georgia Tech, but as she sat there in her beige linen business suit, her thick chin dropping into a polka-dotted cravat, he regretted again that she was not the child of his dreams. Babli would be able to help him out moneywise if something happened to him, something so bad that even his pension plans and his insurance policies and his money market schemes wouldn't be enough. But Babli could never comfort him. She wasn't womanly or tender the way that unmarried girls had been in the wistful days of his adolescence. She could sing Hindi film songs, mimicking exactly the high, artificial voice of Lata Mungeshkar, and she had taken two years of dance lessons at Sona Devi's Dance Academy in Southfield, but these accomplishments didn't add up to real femininity. Not the kind that had given him palpitations in Ranchi.

Mr Bhowmick did his best with his wife's French toast. In spite of its filling of marshmallows, apricot jam and maple syrup, it tasted rubbery. He drank two cups of Darjeeling tea, said, 'Well, I'm off,' and took off.

All might have gone well if Mr Bhowmick hadn't fussed longer than usual about putting his briefcase and his trench-coat in the backseat. He got in behind the wheel of his Oldsmobile, fixed his seatbelt and was just about to turn the key in the ignition when his neighbor, Al Stazniak, who was starting up his Buick Skylark, sneezed. A sneeze at the start of a journey brings bad luck. Al Stazniak's sneeze was fierce, made up of five short bursts, too loud to be ignored.

Be careful out there! Mr Bhowmick could see the goddess's scarlet tongue tip wagging at him.

He was a modern man, an intelligent man. Otherwise he couldn't have had the options in life that he did have. He couldn't have given up a good job with perks in Bombay and found a better job with General Motors in Detroit. But Mr Bhowmick was also a prudent enough man to know that some abiding truth lies bunkered within each wanton Hindu superstition. A sneeze was more than a sneeze. The heedless are carried off in ambulances. He had choices to make. He could ignore the sneeze, and so challenge the world unseen by men. Perhaps Al Stazniak had hayfever. For a sneeze to be a potent omen, surely it had to be unprovoked and terrifying, a thunderclap cleaving the summer skies. Or he could admit the smallness of mortals, undo the fate of the universe by starting over, and go back inside the apartment, sit for a second on the sofa, then re-start his trip.

Al Stazniak rolled down his window. 'Everything okay?'

Mr Bhowmick nodded shyly. They weren't really friends in the way neighbors can sometimes be. They talked as they parked or pulled out of their adjacent parking stalls. For all Mr Bhowmick knew, Al Stazniak had no legs. He had never seen the man out of his Skylark.

He let the Buick back out first. Everything was okay, yes, please. All the same he undid his seatbelt. Compromise, adaptability, call it what you will. A dozen times a day he made these small trade-offs between new-world reasonableness and old-world beliefs.

While he was sitting in his parked car, his wife's ride came by. For fifty dollars a month, she was picked up and dropped off by a hard up, newly divorced woman who worked at a florist's shop in the same mall. His wife came out the front door in brown K-Mart pants and a burgundy windbreaker. She waved to him, then slipped into the passenger seat of the florist's rusty Japanese car.

He was a metallurgist. He knew about the rust and ways of preventing it, secret ways, thus far unknown to the Japanese.

Babli's fiery red Mitsubishi was still in the lot. She wouldn't leave for work for another eight minutes. He didn't want her to know he'd been undone by a sneeze. Babli wasn't tolerant of superstitions. She played New Wave music in their tapedeck. If asked about Hinduism, all she'd ever said to her American friends was that 'it's neat.' Mr Bhowmick had heard her on the phone years before. The cosmos balanced on the head of a snake was like a beachball balanced on the snout of a circus seal. 'This Hindu myth stuff,' he'd heard her say, 'is like a series of super graphics.'

He'd forgiven her. He could probably forgive her anything. It was her way of surviving high school in a city that was both native to her, and alien.

There was no question of going back where he'd come from. He hated Ranchi. Ranchi was no place for dreamers. All through his teenage years, Mr Bhowmick had dreamed of success abroad. What form that success would take he had left vague. Success had meant to him escape from the constant plotting and bitterness that wore out India's middle class.

Babli should have come out of the apartment and driven off to work by now. Mr Bhowmick decided to take a risk, to dash inside and pretend he'd left his briefcase on the coffee table.

When he entered the living room, he noticed Babli's spring coat and large vinyl pocketbook on the sofa. She was probably sorting through the junk jewelry on her dresser to give her business suit a lift. She read hints about dressing in women's magazines and applied them to her person with seriousness. If his luck held, he could sit on the sofa, say a quick prayer and get back to the car without her catching on.

It surprised him that she didn't shout out from her bedroom, 'Who's there?' What if it had been a rapist?

Then he heard Babli in the bathroom. He heard unladylike squawking noises. She was throwing up. A squawk, a spitting, then the horrible gurgle of a waterfall.

A revelation came to Mr Bhowmick. A woman vomiting in the privacy of the bathroom could mean many things. She was coming down with the flu. She was nervous about a meeting. But Mr Bhowmick knew at once that his daughter, his untender, unloving daughter whom he couldn't love and hadn't tried to love, was not, in the larger world of Detroit, unloved. Sinners are everywhere, even in the bosom of an upright, unambitious family like the Bhowmicks. It was the goddess sticking out her tongue at him.

The father sat heavily on the sofa, shrinking from contact with her coat and pocketbook. His brisk, bright engineer daughter was pregnant. Someone had taken time to make love to her. Someone had thought her tender, feminine. Someone even now was perhaps mooning over her. The idea excited him. It was so grotesque and wondrous. At twenty-six Babli had found the man of her dreams; whereas at twenty-six Mr Bhowmick had given up on truth, beauty and poetry and exchanged them for two years at Carnegie Tech.

Mr Bhowmick's tweed-jacket body sagged against the sofa cushions. Babli would abort, of course. He knew his Babli. It was the only possible option if she didn't want to bring shame to the Bhowmick family. All the same, he could see a chubby baby boy on the rug, crawling to his granddaddy. Shame like that was easier to hide in Ranchi. There was always a barren womb and sanctified by marriage that could claim sudden fructifying by the goddess Parvati. Babli would do what she wanted. She was headstrong and independent and he was afraid of her.

Babli staggered out of the bathroom. Damp stains ruined her linen suit. It was the first time he had seen his daughter look ridiculous, quite unprofessional. She didn't come into the living room to investigate the noises he'd made. He glimpsed her shoeless stockinged feet flip-flop on collapsed arches down the hall to her bedroom.

'Are you all right?' Mr Bhowmick asked, standing in the hall. 'Do you need Sinutab?'

She wheeled around. 'What're you doing here?'

He was the one who should be angry. 'I'm feeling poorly too,' he said. 'I'm taking the day off.'

'I feel fine,' Babli said.

Within fifteen minutes Babli had changed her clothes and

left. Mr Bhowmick had the apartment to himself all day. All day for praising or cursing the life that had brought him along with its other surprises an illegitimate grandchild.

It was his wife that he blamed. Coming to America to live had been his wife's idea. After the wedding, the young Bhowmicks had spent two years in Pittsburgh on his student visa, then gone back home to Ranchi for nine years. Nine crushing years. Then the job in Bombay had come through. All during those nine years his wife had screamed and wept. She was a woman of wild, progressive ideas — she'd called them her 'American' ideas — and she'd been martyred by her neighbors for them. American *memsahib. Markin mem, Markin mem.* In bazaars the beggar boys had trailed her and hooted. She'd done provocative things. She'd hired a *chamar* woman who by caste rules was forbidden to cook for higher caste families, especially for widowed mothers of decent men. This had caused a blowup in the neighborhood. She'd made other, lesser errors. While other wives shopped and cooked every day, his wife had cooked the whole week's menu on weekends.

'What's the point of having a refrigerator, then?' She'd been scornful of the Ranchi women.

His mother, an old-fashioned widow, had accused her of trying to kill her by poisoning. 'You are in such a hurry? You want to get rid of me quick-quick so you can go back to the States?'

Family life had been turbulent.

He had kept aloof, inwardly siding with his mother. He did not love his wife now, and he had not loved her then. In any case, he had not defended her. He felt some affection, and he felt guilty for having shunned her during those unhappy years. But he had thought of it then as revenge. He had wanted to marry a beautiful woman. Not being a young man of means, only a young man with prospects, he had had no right to yearn for pure beauty. He cursed his fate and after a while, settled for a barrister's daughter, a plain girl with a wide, flat plank of a body and myopic eyes. The barrister had sweetened the deal by throwing in an all-expenses-paid two years' study at Carnegie Tech to which Mr Bhowmick had been admitted. Those two years had changed his wife from pliant girl to ambitious woman. She wanted America, nothing less.

It was his wife who had forced him to apply for permanent resident status in the U.S. even though he had a good job in Ranchi as a government engineer. The putting together of documents for the immigrant visa had been a long and humbling process. He had had to explain to a chilly clerk in the Embassy that, like most Indians of his generation, he had no birth certificate. He had to swear out affidavits, suffer through police checks, bribe orderlies whose job it was to move his dossier from desk to desk. The decision, the clerk had advised him, would take months, maybe years. He hadn't dared hope that merit might be rewarded. Merit could collapse under bad luck. It was for grace that he prayed.

While the immigration papers were being processed, he had found the job in Bombay. So he'd moved his mother in with his young brother's family, and left his hometown for good. Life in Bombay had been lighthearted, almost fulfilling. His wife had thrown herself into charity work with the same energy that had offended the Ranchi women. He was happy to be in a big city at last. Bombay was the Rio de Janeiro of the East; he'd read that in a travel brochure. He drove out to Nariman Point at least once a week to admire the necklace of Municipal lights, toss coconut shells into the dark ocean, drink beer at the Oberoi-Sheraton where overseas Indian girls in designer jeans beckoned him in sly ways . His nights were full. He played duplicate bridge, went to the movies, took his wife to Bingo nights at his club. In Detroit he was a lonelier man.

Then the green card had come through. For him, for his wife, and for his daughter who had been born to them in Bombay. He sold what he could sell, and put in his brother's informal trust what he couldn't save on taxes. Then he had left for America, and one more start.

All through the week, Mr Bhowmick watched his daughter. He kept furtive notes on how many times she rushed to the bathroom and made hawking, wrenching noises, how many times she stayed late at the office, calling her mother to say she'd be taking in a movie and pizza afterwards with friends.

He had to tell her that he knew. And he probably didn't have much time. She shouldn't be on Slim-Fast in her condition. He had to choose between public shame for the family, and murder.

For three more weeks he watched her and kept his silence. Babli wore shifts to the office instead of business suits, and he liked her better in those garments. Perhaps she was dressing for her young man, not from necessity. Her skin was pale and blotchy by turn. At breakfast her fingers looked stiff, and she had trouble with silverware.

Two Saturdays running, he lost badly at duplicate bridge. His wife scolded him. He had made silly mistakes. When was Babli meeting this man? Where? He must be American; Mr Bhowmick prayed only that he was white. He pictured his grandson crawling to him, and the grandson was always fat and brown and buttery skinned, like the infant Krishna. An American son-in-law was a terrifying notion. Why was she not mentioning men, at least, preparing the way for the major announcement? He listened sharply for men's names, rehearsed little lines like, 'Hello, Bob, I'm Babli's old man,' with a cracked little laugh. Bob, Jack, Jimmy, Tom. But no names surfaced. When she went out for pizza and a movie it was with the familiar set of Indian girls and their strange, unpopular, American friends, all without men. Mr Bhowmick tried to be reasonable. Maybe she had already gotten married and was keeping it secret. 'Well Bob, you and Babli sure had Mrs Bhowmick and me going there, heh-heh,' he mumbled one night with Sahas and Ghosals, over cards. 'Pardon?' asked Pronob Saha. Mr Bhowmick dropped two tricks, and his wife glared. 'Such stupid blunders,' she fumed on the drive back. A new truth was dawning; there would be no marriage for Babli. Her young man probably was not so young and not so available. He must be already married. She must have yielded to passion or been raped in the office. His wife seemed to have noticed nothing. Was he a murderer, or a conspirator? He kept his secret from his wife; his daughter kept her decision to herself.

Nights, Mr Bhowmick pretended to sleep, but as soon as his wife began her snoring – not real snores so much as loud, gaspy gulpings for breath – he turned on his side and prayed to Kali-Mata.

In July, when Babli's belly had begun to push up against the waistless dresses she'd bought herself, Mr Bhowmick came out of the shower one weekday morning and found the two women screaming at each other. His wife had a rolling pin in one hand. His daughter held up a *National Geographic* as a shield for her head. The crazy look that had been in his wife's eyes when she'd shooed away beggar kids was in her eyes again.

'Stop it!' His own boldness overwhelmed him. 'Shut up! Babli's pregnant, so what? It's your fault, you made us come to the States.'

Girls like Babli were caught between the rules, that's the point he wished to make. They were too smart, too impulsive for a backward place like Ranchi, but not tough nor smart enough for sex-crazy places like Detroit.

'My fault?' his wife cried. 'I told her to do hanky-panky with boys? I told her to shame us like this?'

She got in one blow with the rolling pin. The second glanced off Babli's shoulder and fell on his arm which he had stuck out for his grandson's sake.

'I'm calling the police,' Babli shouted. She was out of the rolling pin's range. 'This is brutality. You can't do this to me.'

'Shut up! Shut your mouth, foolish woman.' He wrenched the weapon from his wife's fist. He made a show of taking off his shoe to beat his wife on the face.

'What do you know? You don't know anything.' She let herself down slowly on a dining chair. Her hair, curled overnight, stood in wild whorls around her head. 'Nothing.'

'And you do!' He laughed. He remembered her tormentors, and laughed again. He had begun to enjoy himself. Now *he* was the one with the crazy, progressive ideas.

'Your daughter is pregnant, yes,' she said, 'any fool knows that. But ask her the name of the father. Go ask.'

He stared at his daughter who gazed straight ahead, eyes

burning with hate, jaw clenched with fury.

'Babli?'

'Who needs a man?' she hissed. 'The father of my baby is a bottle and a syringe. Men louse up your lives. I just want a baby. Oh don't worry – he's a certified fit donor. No diseases, college graduate, above average, and he made the easiest twenty-five dollars of his life –'

'Like animals,' his wife said. For the first time he heard horror in her voice. His daughter grinned at him. He saw her tongue, thick and red, squirming behind her row of perfect teeth.

'Yes, yes, yes,' she screamed, 'like livestock. Just like animals. You should be happy – that's what marriage is all about, isn't it? Matching bloodlines, matching horoscopes, matching castes, matching, matching, matching…' and it was difficult to know if she was laughing or singing, or mocking and like a madwoman.

Mr Bhowmick lifted the rolling pin high above his head and brought it down hard on the dome of Babli's stomach. In the end, it was his wife who called the police.

S phinxes

There was a knock early one evening at Mr Hovsepian's front door. A girl was standing there, aged about twenty and dressed all in blue. Her lightweight cotton jacket matched her blue skirt and her cotton blouse was a little lighter. Her eyes, too, were blue, and around her neck she wore a blue tie.

She had long fair hair that fell to below her shoulders. In her left hand she held a clipboard with a pad of paper clipped to it. In her right was a biro. A bulging canvas satchel hung from one shoulder. Her smile was bright and disarming.

'Hello, I've come for your form.'

Mr Hovsepian, short, portly, bald and middle-aged gazed at her and blinked rapidly several times. 'I beg your pardon?'

'Your form,' the girl repeated. 'Your questionnaire.'

Mr Hovsepian was at a loss. He shrugged and smiled apologetically, saying, 'I am sorry, I do not know what this is.'

The girl said, 'I put one through your door a week ago. You're supposed to fill it in and have it ready for me to collect this evening.'

Mr Hovsepian shook his head.

'I did not receive your form,' he said. 'I am sorry. I am afraid I do not have one for you.'

61

Behind the girl, on the other side of the street, he saw a woman with a clipboard and satchel. She was at the door of one of his neighbours. The neighbour, Mrs Boyle, was handing a large green form to the woman. Seeing Mr Hovsepian she waved briefly then disappeared back indoors.

Mr Hovsepian leaned forward slightly and peered up and down the street. There were several people in view, male and female, all bearing clipboards and satchels. They all appeared to be collecting forms.

The girl in blue looked crestfallen.

'Oh dear,' she said. 'You're not going to be difficult, are you? I've had so many already. They get so grumpy and it isn't my fault. And I'm supposed to have all the forms in by tomorrow.'

'Oh no, I do not wish to be difficult,' Mr Hovsepian said anxiously, chiding himself for having caused distress to such a pretty girl. 'Please do not think that. It is just that I do not have one of these forms. What are they for?'

'Oh it's just a simple questionnaire,' the girl told him. Her smile returned and her manner was buoyant once more. 'We just need a few details for our records. Don't worry, it's all strictly private and confidential. Just statistics and that sort of thing, you know. Perhaps if I were to give you one now you could fill it in for me and I'll call back for it tomorrow?'

'Certainly, I would be delighted!' Mr Hovsepian beamed at the girl, happy that he had made her smile again.

'In fact, I could even take down a few details right now, Mr...?'

'Hovsepian,' Mr Hovsepian said. He adjusted his black rimmed spectacles and twisted his neck in order to get a better view of what the girl was writing. He wondered, fleetingly, if he had done the right thing in giving her his name. After all, one never knows.

The girl's perfume drifted into his nostrils and he lost his train of thought.

'And are you the owner of these premises, Mr Hovsepian?'

He hesitated. 'No. It is council owned.'

'And what is your marital status?'

'I am a widower. My wife died some time ago.'

'Children?'

62

'No, none. I am alone.'

'Oh, that's wonderful, then!' the girl cried, her face bright with smiles and dimples. 'It will take you no time at all to fill it in! Now, where are we....?'

She delved into her satchel and pulled out a green foolscap sized form, several pages in length, which she wrote on and handed to Mr Hovsepian.

Just then a man appeared at her side.

'Any trouble?' he asked curtly. There was an air of official-dom about him that Mr Hovsepian was immediately con-scious of. He was tall and aloof, dressed in a plain brown jac-ket with leather patches at the elbow, light grey, razor-creased trousers, and brown brogues. His short silver hair had begun to thin and he sported neatly trimmed sideburns. He sur-veyed Mr Hovsepian cooly, almost insultingly.

'No, no problems,' the girl replied. 'This gentleman seems to have mislaid his form, but I've given him another one. It just means I'll have to call back again tomorrow, that's all.'

The man's jaw muscles quivered.

'What's your name?' he demanded.

Mr Hovsepian was taken aback and did not immediately reply.

'Mr Hovsepian,' the girl put in for him. A few of the other collectors had gathered behind her and the man in the brown jacket. They looked on inquisitively. Their satchels were full and they held their clipboards loosely at their sides.

The man in the brown jacket said, 'Mr Hopsemian, it states here at the top of page one' – he jabbed Mr Hovsepian's form with an index finger – 'that this form will be collected today. It specifically requests that you have the completed form ready for collection. Now, everyone else in this street, everyone in this dis-trict in fact, has complied with this request. Why not you?'

'But I did not receive this form!' Mr Hovsepian protested, thoroughly disconcerted. 'How can I fill it in when I do not have it?'

'You weren't trying to be awkward, were you, Mr Horste-pian?'

'No. I know nothing about this form. Nobody has told me anything about it.'

The man drew back his head and peered down his nose at Mr Hovsepian. 'Hmm.' He turned to the others. 'All right, that's enough. Let's be off.'

As they moved away, perhaps a dozen in all, he leaned close to Mr Hovsepian and said, 'I feel I ought to remind you, Mr Opsetrian, that you are required by law to complete this form. It will be to your advantage to do so. Goodnight.'

Mr Hovsepian caught the gleam of two gold teeth and a strong whiff of cologne.

The girl in blue smiled shyly and said, 'I'll call back about midday, Mr Hovsepian.'

She was a very pleasant young lady and Mr Hovsepian looked forward to seeing her again. He hoped, though , that she would turn up minus her truculent companion.

He watched them until they disappeared around the corner at the end of the street then, shaking his head, went indoors. In the living-room he settled himself into his favourite arm-chair and began to study the green form.

On the left hand side of each page of the form a series of questions was printed, one below the other. On the right were white boxes for the answers. There was a white box for each person resident in the household. There were six white boxes for each question. As Mr Hovsepian lived on his own he had only to fill in his answers in the first box.

The questions were arranged numerically from one to one hundred and thirty eight. The form was fifteen pages long.

Mr Hovsepian scanned the pages for some indication of who had devised the questionnaire, but he drew a blank. However, it was stipulated on the first page that completion of the questionnaire was compulsory and that refusal to do so would result in a heavy fine or even imprisonment. The giving of false information, it said, was also an offence that could lead to litigation.

Midway down page one there was a note in bold black capitals to the effect that all information given would be treated in strictest confidence. This did nothing to allay Mr Hovsepian's growing sense of disquiet.

He read the questions one by one. The first questions had to do with his home: what it comprised, whether it had indoor or outdoor toilet facilities, whether it was rented or leased etc. The form went on to enquire as to Mr Hovsepian's date of birth, full name and address, sex, and other related items. Several of these had already been filled in by the girl in blue.

So far so good, but the questions then turned to the state of his finances. This made him stop and ponder. Surely his money was his own affair? He let his eyes roam over each page and he noticed that, as the questions progressed, they were gradually assuming a more and more intimate flavour. The form was cunningly contrived and it was conceivable, Mr Hovsepian saw, that anyone not fully alert, or even too apathetic to care, could quite easily fill in the answer to each question in turn without realizing exactly how much they were revealing about themselves.

By the time he reached the foot of page eight Mr Hovsepian was seriously troubled.

'Good Lord!' he murmured to himself. 'Good Lord! Good-Lord!'

At the bottom of page twelve he let the form drop into his lap. He sat with one elbow resting on the arm of his chair and began to chew distractedly with his lips on the knuckle of his forefinger. He thought long and hard, and with increasing nervousness. At length he raised himself from the armchair.

'This is diabolical!' he exclaimed out loud. 'They cannot do this!'

He left the room, the decision having been taken to pay a call on Desmond, his next-door-neighbour, and seek his opinion on this matter.

Desmond was a classless, ponderous, docile fellow who smelled of Brylcreem and petrol. He was thirty-five, unemployed, and shared his house with a wife and three refractory children. He answered Mr Hovsepian's knock wearing old blue overalls and brown slippers, a can of pale ale clasped loosely in one hand.

'Hello, Mr Hovsepian,' he said with a good-natured grin. 'What can I do for you?'

The smell of cooking wafted out from behind him and the television blasted in the interior of the house. Two children came thundering down the stairs, shouting wildly and waving their arms about their heads. As they chased out of the door one of them landed Mr Hovsepian a passing thwack in the testicles, causing him to cry out sharply in pain. Desmond appeared not to have noticed.

'I came to ask you about these forms we have all been given,' Mr Hovsepian gasped, endeavouring to ignore his discomfort.

'Yeah?' Desmond stretched his lips, leaned a massive forearm against the door-frame, and began to pick at his teeth with a grubby fingernail. 'What forms are they then?'

'The questionnaires. The ones we have all had to fill in. You must have had one?'

Desmond looked dubious. 'Don't know about that. 'Spect Doreen saw to all that.' He leaned back and called into the house, 'Dot!'

The answer rode back over the din of the television. 'What?'

'Know anything about some forms?'

'I gave 'em back earlier this evenin.'

'Yes I know,' Mr Hovsepian called. 'But I was just wondering what you thought of some of the questions they asked. Didn't you think they were of a rather private nature? Were you not outraged at some of the personal details demanded in them?'

There was a short silence, then: 'Yeah, I was a bit, I suppose.'

Another pause followed then she called out, 'Who's that, Des?'

'It's Mr Hovsepian. He's a bit upset about the forms.'

Doreen's head appeared at the living room door. 'Hello, Mr Hovsepian,' she said and ducked back inside.

'Well, I think some of them are most impertinent!' Mr Hovsepian declared.

'Personally I don't know anythin about it,' Desmond told him. 'Never even saw 'em.'

'But do you not think that it is a gross infringement of basic civil liberties to insist that we answer such questions? Do you not feel we have a right to refuse? I mean, there are some things that are personal and confidential and that nobody else has a right to know about. We should stand up for ourselves!

For our rights and our beliefs!'

Desmond pushed his jaw forward and grimaced towards the roof of a house across the road.

'Yeah, I suppose so,' he said, then added forlornly, 'Still, what can you do?'

Mr Hovsepian gave up.

'Well thank you, Desmond,' he said with complete sincerity. 'Thank you very much indeed.'

'Pleasure, Mr Hovsepian,' Desmond said and stepped back inside.

Mr Hovsepian, deeply concerned, felt inclined to call on Ella, the plump Jamaican divorcee who lived next door on the other side. As he was approaching her door though, a motorbike pulled up outside. A youth in jeans and leather dismounted, strode up to the house and rang her doorbell. A moment later, as Mr Hovsepian watched, the door opened and Ella appeared. With a cry of delight she flung her arms around the young man and pulled him inside. The door shut loudly behind her.

Mr Hovsepian went home.

At eleven-thirty the following morning the girl in blue was standing smiling at Mr Hovsepian's door. She was dressed as she had been the previous day and the sun glinted off her golden hair. She was very lovely; Mr Hovsepian wondered if he dared ask her in for a cup of tea.

'Hello, Mr Hovsepian,' she beamed, showing her even white teeth, 'do you have the form for me?'

Mr Hovsepian was suddenly overcome with contrition. He had been so embroiled with the thought of upholding his dignity in what he considered to be a grave moral and social issue, that he had barely given a thought to how his conduct might affect the girl. He looked past her and fumbled in the pockets of his trousers.

'Well,... no,' he said with difficulty.

A silence followed during which he was unable to look her in the face. He found, to his embarrassment, that he was staring at her legs – which were very shapely – and he shifted his gaze quickly to the solitary milk bottle on the doorstep.

'No?' the girl asked at length. 'But Mr Hovsepian, why?'

Her voice speared him. He knew he had hurt her. It was possible she could even lose her job because of him. Nevertheless, it was imperative that he stick to his guns. She was no doubt too young to see just what an important issue this was.

'Have you read this questionnaire?' he asked her. 'Have you seen some of the questions that are contained in it? They have no right to expect answers to these questions. A man must be allowed to enjoy a certain amount of privacy.'

'But I have read the questionnaire,' the girl replied, 'and I've not seen anything on it that could possibly cause offence. Of course you have the right to privacy, we all do, but as far as I can see the questions are all quite innocuous. And anyway,' she smiled reassuringly, 'you don't have to worry, it's all strictly private and confidential.'

Mr Hovsepian shook his head. 'How can you be working for them, a nice girl like you?'

He raised his eyes now, bravely, and looked into hers. She looked away demurely.

'This cannot be law,' he said. 'It is not just. Who are they, these anonymous persons who wish to know so much about us all? Who are they Miss, you should not work for them. You really should not.'

He was going to invite her in then – he almost did it – but shyness claimed him. He fell silent and dropped his gaze again. His eyes shifted of their own accord to her ankles and he felt a little tingle somewhere deep inside him. All his life he had ached for a girl like this one.

Another pair of legs appeared then alongside those of the girl. Shining brown brogues covered the feet, and above them the immaculately creased light grey trousers. Mr Hovsepian looked up. The Man In The Brown Jacket glowered at him.

'There's always one, isn't there!' he said with utmost contempt. 'You can bet your bloody life that there's always going to be one!'

Mr Hovsepian's head jerked back several inches on his shoulders and one eye shut tight – his involuntary method of displaying the fact that not only had he been caught completely unawares, but that he was also severely shocked.

Unfortunately, and as he was all too aware, the expression produced was something rather comical. In the past people had been known to laugh outright at the sight.

He squinted, speechless, at The Man In The Brown Jacket. Later, he knew, he would think of a score of artful and belittling rebuttals with which to put The Man well and truly in his place, but for now he was struck mute.

The man was paying him no further direct attention. Both he and the girl in blue had begun writing on the clipboards they carried. As they wrote their eyes swept over the facade of Mr Hovsepian's house. They peered beyond him into the interior and they looked him up and down and scribbled brief notes.

'What are you doing?' Mr Hovsepian demanded anxiously, finding his tongue again. 'What is it you are writing?'

Neither one answered. The girl did look up – and he thought he saw sympathy in her eyes – but she didn't speak. It was possible that she was about to say something to him but a searing glance from her companion ensured her silence.

Mr Hovsepian took a deep breath.

'Who are you people?' he demanded. 'Who do you work for?'

There was no reply.

'You cannot go around behaving like this, treating people in this manner! It is immoral! It is an invasion of privacy! There are certain things a person does not disclose to all and sundry – to anybody for that matter. You have no right to show such disrespect and you have no right to pry!'

They stopped writing. The Man looked at him and nodded to himself. 'Oh, so you have secrets, do you?' he asked with knowing disdain.

Mr Hovsepian grew flustered. He wondered what he had revealed.

'Mr Hovsepian,' the girl in blue said gently, 'everybody else has filled their forms in. You really don't have anything to gain by being obstinate.'

There was patience and condolement in her voice. Mr Hovsepian felt great affinity for her. He really could not understand how she had come to be engaged in such an unsavoury occupation.

'Nevertheless,' he declared defiantly, determined not to be humiliated in front of her again, 'it is an infringement of basic civil liberties.'

'Pah!' The Man guffawed.

Mr Hovsepian's head shot back again, but this time he did not squint.

'How dare you! I will have you know that I have lived in this house for more than nine years and never before –' he stopped short. Both The Man and the girl resumed writing.

'Carry on,' the Man urged, not looking up, 'don't let us distract you.'

Mr Hovsepian was dumbfounded. He looked from one to the other of them and sweat broke out above his upper lip.

'Yes?' The Man coaxed. 'You were saying?'

Mr Hovsepian grabbed the door. 'I have never known anything like this!' he declared. 'Let me tell you now that I have no intention whatsoever of filling in your form, and that is all I have to say on the matter!'

With that he slammed the door in their faces.

As he strode back towards his living-room The Man In The Brown Jacket pushed open the flap of the letterbox and called to him, 'Mr Ubscrepiant, I feel that I ought to remind you one more time that the completion of this questionnaire *is* compulsory. *By* law.

'We're off to the local hostelry now to grab a bite of lunch and a little liquid refreshment. Have a think about it. We'll be back in a little while.'

Mr Hovsepian ignored him. He marched into his living-room and sat himself down angrily in his favourite armchair.

Two hours later the door knocker sounded. Mr Hovsepian refused to acknowledge it.

He went to the window and looked out. The Man and the girl were standing outside his front door. Parked at the side of the road in front of the house was a dark green Bedford van. The rear doors were open and inside Mr Hovsepian recognized the collectors who had accompanied The Man and the girl on the previous day.

The girl in blue saw him standing at the window.

'Mr Hovsepian, please be reasonable,' she implored him. 'Please come to the door.'

Much as he felt disinclined Mr Hovsepian did not have it in him to ignore her entreaties. In his heart he sensed that she was basically good. Somehow she had gotten herself mixed up with the wrong crowd, that was all. It was not her fault. She was young and gullible, easily led. He saw it as his duty to try and help her; it would be churlish of him to do otherwise.

So he opened the door.

The girl smiled warmly at him. The Man surveyed him with narrowed eyes.

'We've come to collect your completed questionnaire, Mr Miscrepiant,' The Man said between his teeth. 'Is it ready and waiting for us?'

Mr Hovsepian rather courageously ignored him. He turned to the girl.

'M-my dear,' he began, taking a deep breath, 'I can see how, what with the soaring unemployment statistics, the current economic climate, the decline in job opportunities, and so forth…, one may be obliged of necessity to accept an offer of employment to which one is not wholly suited. I sympathize with you deeply, truly I do, but I feel I must warn you about the situation you have allowed yourself to fall into,' – he glanced at The Man In The Brown Jacket, feeling himself running out of steam – 'You are in grave danger, Miss. I would very much like to think that there is something I can do to help.'

The girl gazed at him wonderingly as he spoke. When he stopped she glanced nervously at her superior.

'There is,' The Man said. 'You can stop acting like the little foreign creep that you are and bloody well fill in your questionnaire!'

'I am not foreign!' Mr Hovsepian stamped one foot indignantly. The desired effect was lost due to his spectacles slipping down the length of his nose, which was shiny with perspiration. He caught them at the tip with one hand, adding somewhat disconcertedly, 'I was born here in this country and not once have I even stepped beyond its shores.'

The Man and the girl were writing furiously once more. Mr Hovsepian fell into exasperated silence, unable to express his emotions.

At length The Man let go of his pen, which fell dangling on a string attached to his clipboard, and fixed him with a steady, sardonic gaze.

'You know, if you had only filled in your questionnaire as you were supposed to – as everyone else did – you would not have had to put up with the embarrassment of having to explain yourself like this, for I would not have made such an error. You really are very silly.' He picked up his pen again and, glancing down the page, said, 'I believe it is safe to assume that your father, at least, was of continental extraction?'

A small muscle twitched just above Mr Hovsepian's upper lip.

'Why do you have to keep bothering me?' he asked, his voice tremulous. 'Why don't you just go away and let me be?'

'Impossible!' The Man snapped.

Keeping his eyes on Mr Hovsepian, almost with amusement, he turned his head slightly in the direction of the Bedford van, raised his hand and clicked his fingers. Immediately the van emptied itself of its human cargo.

They lined up in a double row on the pavement, ten of them, each one armed with a clipboard and pen.

'Now then, for the last time, Mr Excremiant,' The Man In The Brown Jacket said, 'will you or will you not hand back your completed questionnaire?'

Mr Hovsepian stood firm. 'I will not!' he pronounced with dignity. He stepped back inside, took hold of the door and once more closed it in their faces.

From inside his living room he heard The Man bark out a couple of musket-shot commands. This was followed by the sounds of dispersing feet. Then the noise began.

They banged on the door with flats of hands, sides of fists and bare knuckles. They rat-a-tat-tatted the metal door knocker. Two faces appeared at the window. They called to Mr Hovsepian and tapped and thudded on the pane.

'Go away!' Mr Hovsepian shouted furiously. 'Go away! Go away!'

He jumped up and closed the curtains.

'Mr Hovsepian!' It was the voice of the girl in blue calling to him through the letterbox. 'Please don't be so obstinate, Mr Hovsepian. It really won't help matters, and we're only trying to do our job.'

Mr Hovsepian experienced a pang of remorse. He went into the hall. He could see the girl's wide blue eyes staring at him through the letterbox.

'My dear, I have no desire to cause you personally any inconvenience or aggravation, please understand that. But I consider it my moral duty to stand up for my rights as a citizen of this country. In this I am afraid I am unbendable.'

'But Mr Hovsepian, one of the conditions implicit in holding the status of a citizen of this country is that you adhere to its laws. And one of these laws states that all citizens must complete this questionnaire. It's all dealt with in the strictest confidence, you needn't worry.'

Mr Hovsepian opened his mouth to reply, but at that moment he heard a noise behind him, in the kitchen.

He rushed in there to find the doors of two cabinets wide open. Crouched in front of them was a man. He was peering into the interior of the cabinets and busily jotting down notes on a pad attached to the clipboard he held.

'What on earth!' Mr Hovsepian swooped on the man, slamming the cabinet doors shut as he did so. 'What are you doing in here? How did you get in?'

The man looked up at him in surprise.

'Through there!' He indicated the back door with a jerk of his thumb.

'You mean you just walked in, uninvited?'

'I was told to,' the man replied in a peeved tone. 'I'm only doin me job.' He rose, brushed past Mr Hovsepian and opened the door of another cupboard, began taking notes.

Mr Hovsepian leapt forward and slammed the door shut. 'Get out! Get out! There are things in there you have no right knowing about!'

'Oh yeah?' The man was suddenly curious, his pen poised.

'What kind of things?'

'Well, I – I –' Mr Hovsepian spluttered. There *were* things in there, he knew, but for the life of him he could not remember what. 'That is none of your business!' He steered the man towards the door. 'You have no right being here. Get out!'

As he pushed the man out he saw two women and another man standing in his back garden. All three were jotting down notes. He closed the door and leaned against it. His shirt was damp and clung to his dumpy form.

Meanwhile the noise at the front was continuing unabated. The Man In The Brown Jacket was shouting sarcastic remarks through the letterbox and someone was still banging on the living-room window.

'I shall call the police!' Mr Hovsepian yelled.

The Man laughed.

Mr Hovsepian wondered about the police. He had no telephone in the house. The nearest was a public call box at the end of the street. He was extremely reluctant to leave the house, knowing that to do so would mean leaving everything he owned, his most personal and private possessions, at the mercy of his aggressors.

He was jerked from this train of thought by a sudden scraping sound above his head. In disbelief he raced headlong up the stairs to the back bedroom. A man and a woman were in there, both taking notes.

'My God!'

He stood gaping in the centre of the room. The intruders looked up and smiled briefly, then turned back to their tasks. The man stood on a chair and investigated the top of Mr Hovsepian's wardrobe; the woman slid open a drawer and began to rifle through its contents. Mr Hovsepian leapt in front of the woman, between her and the chest of drawers.

'You have no right to be looking in there! Get out this instant!'

'Oh but we can't,' the woman protested. 'We haven't finished yet.'

Mr Hovsepian, terrified at the thought of what they might already have unearthed, fought to clear his thoughts. He noted the open window and, leaning against the outer sill, the two aluminium stocks of an extending ladder. Beyond and below him, in the garden next door, he saw Desmond. He rushed to the window.

Desmond was sitting backwards on a child's red three-wheeler, hacking drowsily with a blunt hatchet at a large block of wood.

'Desmond!' Mr Hovsepian called, his voice shaking with emotion. 'Desmond!'

Desmond looked up from his pastime but seemed to experience difficulty in locating the source of the voice that hailed him. Mr Hovsepian called again and this time Desmond found him. He grinned roguishly and waved a hand.

'Hello, Mr Hovsepian. How are you?'

'Desmond, please, I have to ask a favour of you. I want you to go down to the telephone kiosk and call the police. Tell them – tell them I'm being invaded.'

Desmond stood up slowly. His wide brow slid forward to obscure his eyes for a moment in a puzzled frown. 'Invaded,' he said to himself tonelessly.

'Yes, please, Desmond! It's of utmost urgency!'

Desmond looked up at him again and smiled. 'All right, Mr Hovsepian. I'll go now if you like.'

Happy to have found a mission in life he set off out of the garden and down the narrow path that ran along the rear of the houses. Mr Hovsepian turned to face the couple in his bedroom.

'The police will be here in a minute,' he said. 'I would advise you to leave immediately.'

'I don't think there was any need for that,' the woman said, sliding open a second drawer. 'We're only following orders, after all.'

'Whose orders?' Mr Hovsepian demanded, closing the drawer again.

'It's the Law needs changing!' Mr Hovsepian declared angrily. 'Now please *get out!*'

Muttering to themselves the two clambered out of the window and down the ladder.

As he was putting the latch on the window Mr Hovsepian heard a voice hailing him from outside.

'Mr Hovsepian! Mr Hovsepian!' It was Desmond. 'Have you got a 10p for the telephone? I haven't got any.'

Mr Hovsepian rummaged in his trouser-pockets.

'No I haven't.'

Desmond looked forlorn.

'Desmond, this is an emergency!' Mr Hovsepian shouted. 'You do not need any money. Just dial 999!'

Desmond's face brightened.

'All right, Mr Hovsepian,' he said, and set off again at a slightly brisker pace.

Downstairs they were still knocking at the front door – a regular, persistent rapping now, calculated to have an effect, Mr Hovsepian perceived, comparable to that of the Chinese water torture.

Approximately five minutes later two policemen drew up outside in a red unmarked saloon. Mr Hovsepian opened the door to them gratefully.

'Now then, sir,' the first officer said by way of greeting, 'what seems to be the trouble?'

He bore the stripes of a sergeant and was a big, fatherly, grey-haired man aged about fifty – something that Mr Hovsepian found reassuring. His companion, by complete contrast, was young, taut and cocksure. His cheeks had a permanent flush and he chewed with haughty insolence on a piece of gum. His flickering eyes sized Mr Hovsepian up like they would a cockroach.

Mr Hovsepian addressed himself solely to the sergeant.

'These people have unlawfully invaded my home,' he said. The Man In The Brown Jacket, the girl in blue and the others clustered around him and the two policemen, listening. 'They have entered without my permission through doors and windows, they have plundered my possessions, ransacked my house, and caused me a great deal of distress.' He was beginning to grow excited. 'Their conduct is deplorable! I am at my wit's end! They are behaving like animals! No, worse than animals! They are terrorizing me!'

As he was speaking his voice had risen in pitch until it almost cracked. Without being aware of it he had drawn himself up and was balancing on the balls of his feet. Now, having delivered his irate censure, he slumped and fell silent. He stole a glance at the girl in blue. He had not meant to include her amongst the others. He felt unhappy now, concerned that he might have hurt her.

'And you object to this treatment, do you, sir?' the sergeant enquired, slipping a notebook from his breast pocket and licking the tip of his pencil.

'But of course I object to it! Would not you? This is my home, my castle, not a public market place!'

The Young Constable leered cynically at this. He chewed more rapidly on his gum and cold laughter flashed briefly in his eyes.

'No need to take umbrage, sir,' the sergeant said. 'Just trying to ascertain the facts.'

'If I might elucidate a little here, sergeant,' The Man In The Brown Jacket interposed, 'this – ahem – gentleman, has refused adamantly and repeatedly to complete this official questionnaire. In order to obtain the information that the law demands I found myself obliged to instruct my colleagues to enter his house. He was warned several times beforehand that if he did not yield the information voluntarily it would be taken from him by other means.'

The sergeant's expression changed slightly. He turned back to Mr Hovsepian. 'Is this so?'

'Indeed it is. I am protecting my rights as a citizen of this country. I shall take it to the High Court if necessary.'

The young constable grinned. The sergeant sighed and shook his head tiredly, nodded to The Man In The Brown Jacket and stepped aside to leave the doorway clear. The Man, in turn, signalled to his cohort. They began to enter the house once more, this time through the front door, filing one by one past Mr Hovsepian and the two policemen.

'But – but –' Mr Hovsepian began. The girl in blue passed him. She gave him a sorrowful look. The young constable's eyes followed her down the hallway.

'Now then, sir,' The Sergeant said gruffly, 'let's have a few details, shall we? Name? Address?'

'But this cannot be right!' Mr Hovsepian blubbered.

'Well, I'm afraid it is,' the Sergeant replied. 'These people are acting perfectly within the law and you are committing a criminal offence by attempting to obstruct them. Now, details, please.'

Mr Hovsepian was crushed. The inconceivable had happened: his home was no longer his. All that he considered sacred was being laid bare for the world to see. Delving strangers filled his house, prying into his most personal affairs, dragging out his skeletons from their shadowy, half-forgotten recesses, disinterring his sphinxes...As he gave The Sergeant the details he demanded his mind filled with fear.

The Young Constable swaggered past them, down the hall and into the kitchen where the girl in blue was taking notes. He said something to her that Mr Hovsepian didn't catch then swaggered back, grinning to himself and slapping the palm of one hand with his truncheon.

Mr Hovsepian looked imploringly at The Sergeant.

'Surely there must be something I can do?' he cried.

'Yeah, there is,' The Young Constable said from where he now stood in the doorway. His back was to Mr Hovsepian and he was looking out at the street. 'You can move out.'

The Man In The Brown Jacket, who was leaning against the wall a couple of yards away and taking in the proceedings, gave a low chuckle. Mr Hovsepian squinted.

'What does he mean?' he asked The Sergeant.

'He's just having a joke,' The Sergeant replied, 'but in a manner of speaking what he says is true. You have refused to give the information that the law says you must give, so these people have 'invaded' your home, as you put it. There isn't a thing you can do about that. Were things a little different, however, were you for instance to be homeless, then they could not invade your home, could they, because you wouldn't have a home for them to invade.

'Pure logic, really – in a roundabout way.'

Mr Hovsepian fell back. The Sergeant turned to The Man In The Brown Jacket. 'Do you want us to book him, sir?'

The Man shook his head. 'Nah. I don't think he'll give us any more trouble.'

A sudden jubilant yell rang out from upstairs. 'Whoo! Look

what I've found!'

The Man In The Brown Jacket looked upwards and smiled. The Young Constable leered and chewed his gum with his incisors. The Sergeant put away his notepad. Mr Hovsepian hid his face in his hands.

'Well, if there's nothing else I suppose we'll be getting along,' The Sergeant said. 'Good-day, gents.'

There was another whoop from upstairs followed by a series of giggles and guffaws.

Mr Hovsepian could not think. For the life of him he could not remember what it was they might have found. Nevertheless he knew himself to be exposed.

'Please,' he said to The Man In The Brown Jacket, 'can I have five minutes to be alone?'

The Man scowled. 'I don't see any reason why you should. You've delayed us by two days already.'

The girl in blue appeared at his side. She gazed sadly at Mr Hovsepian then turned to The Man and laid a hand lightly on his arm. Her expression seemed to communicate something to him, something that caused him to relent.

'Very well,' he said. 'Tell whoever is in your way to leave you alone for five minutes. But no longer!'

Mr Hovsepian made his way upstairs to his bedroom. Two people were in there, a woman in her twenties and a man a few years older. They turned their flushed faces away as he entered. Mr Hovsepian gave them The Man's instructions and they left. He closed the door behind them.

He emerged five minutes later wearing a pale brown mac and lugging a heavy brown suitcase. The girl in blue was on the landing, checking the contents of his airing-cupboard. She turned to face him as he passed.

'I'm sorry, Mr Hovsepian,' she said. 'I feel somehow responsible for this, as though it's all my fault.'

'No, please do not think that,' Mr Hovsepian told her. 'I would not want you to feel that way. I know that this has nothing to do with you. I understand.'

He inhaled deeply. He was about to try to tell her how much he liked her but the voice of The Man In The Brown Jacket came barking up the stairs and cut rudely between them. 'Mr Homoseparant! Time's up!'

Mr Hovsepian sighed. 'Well, good-bye,' he said. He offered her a trembling hand.

Her hand as it slipped into his was tiny and soft and warm. It seemed to him that she did not rush to withdraw it – or perhaps that was his imagination.

Outside he paused for a moment on the pavement. A motor-bike pulled up outside Ella's house and the same youth he had seen the evening before entered with his own key. Desmond was standing in his doorway, a can of pale ale in one hand. He grinned amiably and raised the can to Mr Hovsepian.

'Hello, Mr Hovsepian. I called the police for you.'

'Yes. Thank you, Desmond.'

'Everythin all sorted out all right now, is it?'

'Well, yes, I suppose you could say that,' Mr Hovsepian said. He took hold of the handle of his heavy suitcase with both hands and began to walk. Desmond took a swig of ale.

'You goin away, Mr Hovsepian?'

'Yes, I'm going away.'

'Oh.'

Mr Hovsepian walked on. Suddenly Desmond was looming at his side. He stopped.

'Well, 'bye then,' Desmond said, shifting awkwardly and holding out a massive hand. Mr Hovsepian put down his case.

'Good-bye, Desmond.'

'I'll say ta-ra to Doreen for you.'

'Yes, do that. Thank you.' He picked up his case again and moved on.

He had reached the end of the street and was on the point of rounding the corner when he heard the sound of hurried footsteps behind him.

'Mr Hovsepian! Mr Hovsepian!' It was the girl in blue.

Mr Hovsepian raised his head, catching his breath as a tiny bud of hope unfolded suddenly inside him. He let go of the suitcase and turned to face her.

She stopped, a trifle breathless, just in front of him.

'Mr Hovsepian, please don't go,' she said, clasping her hands and gazing at him appealingly. 'Don't let us drive you out like this. There's no need. Really, I feel so badly about it. I don't want you to leave.'

Mr Hovsepian shivered ever so slightly.

'What else can I do?' he asked.

'Come back,' the girl in blue said. She held out her hand. 'Come back with me.'

Mr Hovsepian swallowed.

At that moment, back down the street behind the girl, he saw The Man In The Brown Jacket lean out of an upstairs window and look about him. Catching sight of the two on the corner he cupped his hands to his mouth and yelled, 'And don't forget to tell him what we found underneath the bed!'

Mr Hovsepian tottered slightly. His skin turned pale then flushed. The girl raised her hand quickly to her mouth, averting her eyes but failing to completely stifle the giggle that came involuntarily to her lips. She looked back guiltily at Mr Hovsepian.

Mr Hovsepian gazed at the pavement for a moment. Then, as if finally coming to accept something that previously he had been unable to, he straightened. Taking hold of the handle of his heavy brown suitcase with both hands, he turned his back on The Girl In Blue and walked away down the street in the direction of the railway station.

He Said...

He said:

'This is special, so special.'

And he said:

'We're so close, I don't want *anything* to come between us. You can understand that can't you?'

And now, he would not speak to her, would not even come to the phone. But his brother said:

'Why you let him get you pregnant, girl? Don't you know anything at all? What you expect him to do?'

She stood shaking in the phone booth for a long time. Slumped against the dirty glass with the faint smell of urine around her. Realizing that probably some man had walked away from relieving himself, without a backward thought of who had to put up with the results. Just like Errol. A woman in a grey mac tapped on the glass, and on getting no response from Bev, opened the door.

'You all right, dear?'

Bev did not reply, merely shoved her way past, paying no heed to the: 'Some people! No manners at all!' that followed her as she bolted for the sanctuary of her bedsit.

Getting up to her fourth floor room was already becoming

difficult. Her bra was suddenly too tight, her over-sensitive nipples constricted and painful. Halfway up, she became so breathless that she had to stop and sit on the stairs, her head swimming.

She heard feet pounding rapidly down the arch of stairs above her and tried to get up, but her head swam, and when she clung to the bannister it rocked, giving her such a shock that she subsided with a bump. Shocked at the immediacy of her fear for the child, up till then feared and unwanted.

'You okay?'

Bev raised her head and found the woman from the floor below hers looking at her with concern. 'Yes, I'm fine.' She managed a wavery smile.

'You don't look it,' the woman said bluntly.

'I'll be fine. Just a bit dizzy, that's all.' The woman was wearing her uniform, she must be on her way to work. 'Don't let me keep you. I'll be fine,' Bev repeated.

'I'd believe you, if your face wasn't the colour of a ripe avocado,' the woman smiled.

That did it! Bev began to retch violently.

'Oh, shit! I'm sorry!' The woman got to her feet and supported her up the next flight of stairs to their shared bathroom on the landing. Holding her while she retched till her eyes streamed, and her stomach muscles hurt from straining. Then Bev found herself sat down with gentle firmness on the stool, while her face was wiped with a warm face cloth.

Bev opened her eyes tentatively and looked at the woman who was perched on the edge of the bathtub, regarding her critically, the face cloth still in her hand.

'That's not mine,' Bev sniffed and looked towards the rail, 'mine's pink.'

'It's mine.' The woman reached over and tore off some toilet paper which she handed to Bev.

Bev blew her nose, and made a business of disposing of the toilet paper, all the while conscious of the woman's scrutiny. She was feeling better, but still very shaky, and afraid that those eyes watching her so carefully would see straight through to what was really wrong with her. She found that she could not meet the woman's eyes.

'Thank you, I'm alright now,' she muttered ungraciously. 'Don't let me make you late.'

'I've got plenty of time,' the woman said. 'I'll give you a hand up to your room when you're ready.'

'I think I'll stay here for a while,' Bev said hastily, thinking of the state of her room. 'Just in case...' she managed a weak smile.

'Okay,' the woman rinsed and replaced her flannel on the rail, but just as Bev thought she was leaving, she paused in the doorway. 'Have you seen a doctor?'

Bev shook her head, then remembered to add: 'It's nothing, just an upset stomach.' She didn't want it getting back to her parents. She didn't know this woman, but that was not to say that the woman did not know who she was, or know someone who would tell her father.

The woman looked hard at her, then she left, pulling the door to behind her.

Back in her room at last, Bev surrendered to tears. Crying as she had not done since her father had thrown her out. But even that massive rejection had been ameliorated somewhat by the feeling that she was enduring all that for love of Errol, that she had him, and now they could be together. Now, Errol did not want to know her, and her father's predictions looked like coming true. And there was no way back into that fold:

'My daughter is dead!' her father had shouted, while her mother kept quiet and still. 'I have no daughter! As God is my witness! If that harlot crosses my doorstep once more, I will strike her down!' Then he had gone out to a church meeting, leaving her and her silent mother to pack her things.

She had slept on the settee in Mavis's front room for six weeks, till Mavis had suddenly taken a dislike to Errol, and had asked her to leave. Jealousy, Errol had said. But Mavis wouldn't discuss it, just saying that she needed her place to herself, and that it was time they found somewhere else. Finding this room had been like a small miracle, and even though it had taken all the money she had in the Post Office to pay the deposit, she had had such plans when she moved in a month ago.

'What am I going to do?' she asked aloud, rolling over, shading her eyes from the sunglare coming through the high dormer window. 'What am I going to do?' She couldn't think of anyone to call, who would advise her. All the people she knew were either ones that knew her parents, or were Errol's friends, or like Mavis, friends from work.

That reminded her, she hadn't phoned work to tell them she wasn't coming in. She would have to get a doctor's certificate or she would lose her job, even though she wouldn't get paid for the time off.

The thought of work made her feel nauseous. Oh, God! Suppose I can't stand the smell of food? The smell of hamburgers, frying chips, milkshake syrup, seemed to pour out of the walls at her, and she rolled off the bed, wishing she could put her head out of the window, but it was too high. She used the broom to push it open and stood under the cold falling draught of Kilburn air, head back, breathing deeply.

The nausea went away, leaving her feeling thirsty. She made herself some mint tea, and drank it curled in the one armchair, tears running down her face again. Her mother had always made her mint tea when she felt ill. She thought of calling her mother; but instantly rejected the idea. Her mother never kept anything from her father, and Bev had no intention of giving him the satisfaction of being right.

She went along to the surgery along the High Road the next morning, and registered as a patient. It was ironic really, she thought, as she played slow musical chairs towards the doctor's door; she had been intending to come here to see if he would put her on the pill. She had tried her family doctor but he had refused, and had threatened to tell her father if she went anywhere else, saying that the family planning places always notified the GP. Now of course it was too late, had been even before she moved into her room. And Errol must have known, because she hadn't seen him after the first week, and promises of help with the deposit and the rent had never materialized.

'Miss Jordan, is it?' The doctor spoke to the blotter on his desk.

'Jordee, Beverley Jordee,' Bev sat down in the chair on the other side of the desk.

He turned over her new card as if expecting full medical

records to appear magically on the other side. When they did not appear he read her name, age, and address carefully.

'And what seems to be the trouble?' he asked, looking at her for the first time, his face and voice devoid of any desire to know.

'I've not been feeling well, and I've had to stay off work, so...'

'You don't need to see the doctor for a certificate now, you know,' he said brusquely. 'Just see the receptionist and she will give you a form to fill in for yourself.'

His air of dismissal almost swept her from the room, but Bev found herself gripping the edge of the desk, in order not to be swept out.

'I've been sick in the mornings,' she tried a rueful smile; it had no effect. 'Mornings, afternoons, and evenings, actually.'

'Last monthly period?'

Bev gave him the rough approximation that was all that she had because of the irregularity of her periods before.

He grunted. 'Did you bring a sample?' he asked the wall above her head.

'A what?' Did he mean of her sick? Bev wondered.

'A urine sample,' he told the blotter exasperatedly. 'Collect a sample of urine, first thing in the morning, in a *clean* bottle, and bring it to the surgery. The result should be back in a couple of days; phone the receptionist.' He wrote on her new card.

'But the certificate?' Bev asked rather desperately. 'What should I put on the certificate?' She couldn't put the real reason, she needed something medical that meant upset stomach or something like that.

He sighed and drew a pad towards him. 'When did you last work?'

'Tuesday,' Bev said.

'There you are, send the next one in.'

Outside, when she looked at the certificate and saw that he had signed her off work for two weeks, Bev nearly cried. How on earth was she going to manage without pay for two weeks?

Since she had one day to go on her weekly tube pass, Bev decided to take the certificate in and try and placate the manager. She decided, as she walked along, that she didn't really mind the doctor's manner. Old Dr. Saville would have had a fit, and her father would have had a real excuse to kill her then. At least this one didn't give a damn whether she was Pastor Jordee's daughter.

She shivered, and walked a bit faster towards the tube station, trying hard to ignore the babies in pushchairs. What was she going to do? Mavis was the only person that she knew well enough, in her new life, to talk about this. But Mavis was barely speaking to her, and besides, she hated Errol.

So do I! Bev realized, and wanted desperately to be back in the safety of her room, so that she could scream and howl to her heart's content. Then wanted, even more desperately, to go round to Errol's house. To see him, to speak to him.

On the tube, she fantasized. Imagining Errol, holding her tightly in his arms, perhaps his voice breaking with emotion, perhaps a fine tremor in the hand that tenderly wiped away her tears.

I didn't know! He would say. *My brother didn't tell me. He's jealous, because you love me, and he's been in love with you all this while.*

By the time she alighted at Leicester Square, Bev had convinced herself that Barry was making trouble between her and Errol; that Errol didn't really know.

I'll go round there after I've seen the manager at work, and if he's not there, I'll write a letter and post it through the letter box. Mark it Personal and Private.

She felt so much better that she swung in through the door of the burger bar; hope filling her, bearing her forward, like a fair wind in a schooner's sails.

The manager took one harrassed look at her, and his face sketched a lightening perfunctory smile. 'Got a certificate?'

'Yes.' Bev held it out.

'Good!' He made no attempt to take it, or even read it. 'Okay. You relieve Carol on Till Three; have your break an hour later than usual; and if you make up the extra hour today, we'll say no more about it.' All the time he was watching one of the new women mop the floor, and dived off to show her the correct, Company way.

Before she knew it, Bev was changed, and joining the organized chaos behind the counter. Perhaps it was best if she went round Errol's later anyway. He might have found a job, and not be home. Yes, it would be better to go later on, his brother always went to the pub in the evenings.

With this small and overnourished kernel of hope inside her, Bev found that she could cope with work. Sure, when she had her break, she spent it with her swollen feet propped up on a chair, the window wide open beside her, but no one paid any undue attention to this. True, Mavis popped in, and was momentarily concerned, but went away satisfied by Bev's 'First day back!' excuse.

By seven that evening however, Bev was so utterly exhausted that in her thoughts, her high, untidy room, assumed grail-like proportions; attainable only after trial by tube, and stairs. All she wanted was a bath and her bed. Not even her fantasy of a loving Errol, was worth trekking backwards and forwards across London, from the West End to Stoke Newington, and then home to Kilburn.

Her ears were ringing by the time she reached her door, and she just made it into her room before she fainted. When she came to, she lay for a long time on the floor, so utterly miserable that she could not even find tears. She dragged herself onto the bed, kicked off her shoes, knelt up to struggle out of her coat, then lay down and drew the cover over her.

When she woke, it was to bright early sunlight, and a knocking on her open door. Bev started up: Errol! It could be Errol!

'Yes!', she called sitting up so quickly that her head spun.

'Are you alright? It's me, Merle, from downstairs. Can I come in?'

Before Bev could think of an excuse, looking rather wildly around the untidy room, Merle had come in.

'You're not alright, are you?' she came and bent over Bev.

'I was too tired last night,' Bev sketched a hand at her rumpled jumper. 'First day back at work!'

The excuse didn't work with Merle, Bev could see that. Merle straightened, and looked down at Bev. 'When did you last have something to eat?'

Bev, fighting the morning bout of her now, daily nausea, lifted a pleading hand.

'Stay there!' Merle turned briskly away. 'Don't get up,' she ordered, from the doorway.

She was back within a few minutes, a red mug steaming gently in one hand, and a couple of Rich Tea biscuits in the other. She ignored Bev's faint protests and stood over her while she drank the tea, and ate one of the biscuits.

'Thank you,' Bev said finally, handing back the mug to her.

'You'd better see a doctor soon,' she said.

'I went yesterday,' Bev mumbled.

'And?'

Bev wished she would go away, but couldn't find the words to say so. 'I've got to take a sample.'

'Hah!' Merle's laugh was totally devoid of amusement. 'What for? Any woman could tell him what's wrong with you. They can't even take our word for what's happening to us, inside our bodies, can they? They have to have samples...tests.'

On her way to work, later that morning, after dropping off the sample – in an empty pill bottle that Merle located – Bev was uncomfortably aware that she had not thanked Merle properly. She thought of buying her some flowers, or a pot plant, but reasoned herself out of it. One: She could not really afford it. Two: Merle might think that Bev expected her to bring her tea in bed every morning.

The next two days were ordeals to be gotten through somehow, and there was no sign of Merle. Bev made herself a cup of tea, as soon as she got up on the first morning, but it did not ease the queasiness. The next evening she filled a thermos flask with hot water, and placed it next to the bed with a mint teabag ready in a cup. That worked, so at least the day did not start with her head down, over the toilet.

The receptionist's laconic: 'Yes, Miss Jordan, your test was positive. Do you wish to make an appointment to see the doctor?' was no surprise to Bev. She had given up any hope that she wasn't pregnant.

The doctor said: 'Yes, you are pregnant.'

Then he said: 'And the father? Does he know?'

Bev shook her head, and looked down at her hands wrestling with each other in her lap. 'He doesn't want to know.'

'And your parents?'

Bev just shook her head this time.

'Well, what are you going to do? Have you any idea?'

'I don't know,' Bev said, in a voice kept soft, because to speak louder would have revealed her fear and shame; the shame of being unwanted that laid like a cloak about her shoulders. In the romances that she'd borrowed from her friends and read surreptitiously in bed, the coy revelation of a child on the way, had always led to incredulous joy on the man's part as he tenderly took the woman in his arms, as if she were a fragile china doll.

'Do you have a job?' the doctor was asking.

'Yes,' Bev glad for even that small affirmative. 'I work in a burger bar.'

'And have you thought of how you will manage if you have the child?'

'If...?' Bev asked. Surely there was no if about it?

'I could arrange for you to see someone privately.' His hand strayed towards the telephone. 'That would speed things up. You've left it rather late, you know.'

Bev looked blankly at him, she had no idea what he was talking about.

'For a termination...' he looked sharply at her. 'An abortion. If you are to have the pregnancy terminated, we will have to move fast. Will the father help financially, do you think? Or, your parents?'

'An abortion? I don't have to have the baby?' One of her fighting hands disengaged itself to lay flat on her stomach, almost protectively; while the other flew to her cheek, feeling the warmth of hope flaring there.

'If we can get things arranged pretty smartish,' he said.

'Private...? That means I'd have to pay.' Hope died. 'I don't have any money,' Bev said, wishing that she had realized before she paid the deposit on her room.

'No savings?' he said, making it sound like he wasn't really surprised. 'Well I suppose we had better go through the motions of trying for an NHS one. But I don't really hold out much hope. You can't even plead interruption of studies; damaged prospects; that sort of thing, can you?' He shook his head, and tapped his pen on her notes. 'I don't hold out much hope.'

He took some paper out of the wooden stand on his desk and wrote busily for a couple of minutes. Then he sealed the letter carefully in a brown envelope, and pushed it across the desk to her. 'Take that along to the hospital today, and make an appointment to see the consultant. Send the next one in.'

She met Merle on the landing as she was going laboriously up the stairs that evening.

'You sound puffed out,' Merle said. 'Come in and have a cup of tea, or at least a sit down. You look as if you've been climbing Mount Everest.' She took Bev's arm and drew her into her room, depositing her in a chair.

'Why do you always have to put words to my bad feelings?' It came out before she could stop it.

Merle put her head back round the door of her kitchenette, 'It's a talent I have!' she laughed.

'I wouldn't call it a talent exactly,' Bev said, but she had to smile.

She put her bag down on the floor beside her, and unbuttoned her coat. Then she looked round the room. It was bigger than hers, full of plants, and there were pictures and photographs stuck all over the walls. Merle had a proper bed, not just a mattress on the floor, and there was a duvet in a bright yellow cover, and lots of matching pillows.

'Did the doctor give you some iron tablets?' Merle called from the other room. 'You're probably breathless because you're anaemic.' She came back into the room with a tray.

'No, he didn't give me any iron tablets,' Bev said.

'What did he give you then?' Merle placed the tray on the table by Bev, handed her a mug of tea, offered her a plate of coconut macaroons.

Bev's hand began to shake so hard that the tea spilled. 'He gave me a letter to the hospital.' It came out as a grief-stricken wail, surprising and overwhelming her. She had not heard herself make that sort of sound since her gran died. Grief for the death to come, took her, shook her body with deep seismic sobs; touching once again an eight year old's grief for her gran's soft warmth; and the firm voice with the power to temper the harsh edicts of her father's religion.

'Can't go to the Saturday morning pictures with your friends: It's ungodly! Can't wear make-up: It's ungodly! Can't have a baby: It's ungodly!' Bev heard her own voice career out of control, shouting, as she pounded one fist against the wooden arm of the chair.

Then strong warm arms were holding her, and she was rocked, cradled, hushed and soothed; as no one had since her gran died, certainly not her cool, silent, withdrawn mother.

'Is that what you want?' Merle asked her softly, strong arms still enclosing her. 'What you really want?'

'He said it was the best thing,' Bev said into Merle's shoulder.

'Did he really say that?' There was anger in Merle's voice, yet her hands were gentle, stroking Bev's back, smoothing her hair.

'Not in so many words,' Bev admitted. 'But he asked me how I would manage if I had it, and I didn't have any idea...' Little by little she was able to tell Merle exactly what had transpired in the doctor's room, and about her appointment to see the consultant at the hospital in two weeks time.

'But is that what *you* really want?' Merle asked again.

'I don't know!' Bev's hands moved of their own accord, clasping her still flat belly. '*I don't know!*'

'Don't you think that you should take some time to decide?' Merle asked her quietly.

'I haven't *got* time! That's what he said, remember?'

'You've got time,' Merle said with certainty. 'Up until the minute you go into hospital to have it done, you've got the time and the right to think it out; to decide whether it's what you really want.'

'What would you do?' Bev asked.

'I don't know what I'd do in your position,' Merle's voice was calm now, all the anger gone. 'But I would want it to be *my* decision; no one else's. Don't ask me to get involved in making the decision with or for you, I won't do it. All I will say is that you owe it to yourself, to think it through, and make your own decisions. Christ! You would take longer to decide on a new dress than that doctor gave you this morning. I bet he takes longer to decide which *tie* to wear.'

Bev heard footsteps on the stairs. She got carefully out of bed, watching her balance, and wrapped her dressing down around as much of her as it would cover these days. She patted her belly; eight done, and one to go. It was probably Merle. She was due back about now. She usually called up, but if she was silent today, that was not a good sign. Today was the day she did her road test, to see if she could transfer from being a conductor to a driver.

'Merle...?' Bev threw open the door.

'It's me, Baby!' said Errol, standing there in a smart camel coat, driving gloves, and highly polished loafers. 'Or should I say: Babies?' He smiled as his eyes slipped down over her swollen belly.

He removed his gloves as he moved toward her, and Bev backed, speechless, one hand going protectively to her belly.

'You're looking good,' he said, shrugging out of his coat, and laying it carefully over the chair. 'I like your hair in braids: Roots, Baby roots!'

Bev still said nothing, watching his mouth move, smile winningly, while he seemed to use up all the air in her room.

'Barry saw you the other day, and he said you were looking good. And he's right.' Another wide easy smile. 'There's something about a woman when she's carrying your child.'

'*Your child?!*' It came out out as a massive shout that tightened her belly, making the baby kick protestingly. 'This is my child! Nothing to do with you. *Nothing at all!*' Bev swept up his coat and strode out onto the landing. 'Get out of my sight!' She hurled his coat over the banisters, down into the stairwell.

There was a shout from Errol, and a rattle in the stairwell as something fell out of his coat pockets. Then he was pounding down the stairs.

'Hey! Watch it!' Merle shouted from further down the stairs. 'Bev! Bev?' By the sound of it she was taking the stairs two at a time. 'Bev! Are you alright?'

'I'm fine, Merle, fine!' Bev leaned over the rail to call down to her. The front door slammed with a force that reverberated through the house, causing the baby to jump.

Merle paused, breathing hard, on the landing below, and looked up at Bev. 'Well, don't celebrate feeling so fine by falling over the banisters! Come down and celebrate with me. I'm feeling pretty good too.'

'You passed!' Bev went down the stairs.

'Yeah!' Merle threw out her arms and bowed. 'How about a cup of tea to celebrate?' She ushered Bev into her room.

'Can I have hot blackcurrant?'

'It's babies that like that stuff, not their mothers!' Merle said, repeating a joke that had begun when Bev's craving for hot blackcurrent cordial became evident.

'I'm no baby!' Bev said, with some satisfaction, as she arranged most of the pillows on the bed to support her back. 'That's what Errol called me. 'Baby, or should I say: Babies?' Bev mimicked his smooth tones.

'So you threw him out,' Merle gave her her drink, and sat on the end of the bed watching her.

'No, I threw his new coat out!' Bev laughed, one hand going to the baby's kick. 'That upset him much more! I don't think he'll be round again.'

'Do you mind that?'

'Not one bit!' Bev said.

'Will you still not mind, later on?' Merle persisted.

'You never give me any room, do you?' Bev looked down from those searching eyes.

'Fine gestures are great, in the short run,' Merle said, looking soberly down into her mug as if it contained a mirror on time. 'But you have to live with the consequences for a long time. Is that worth a moment's satisfaction?'

'Oh, it was worth it believe me,' Bev said. 'And it wasn't any fine gesture. That was the result of a lot of bad nights. Merle, I have gone from loving him, to hating him, and right out the other side. I don't care what he does, or says anymore. I don't care if I never see him again.'

She looked at Merle, sitting there so contained, staring down into her mug. 'You still don't believe I made the right decision about the abortion, do you?' she challenged that calmness.

'Don't tell me what I think,' Merle said, looking up at her.

'Well somebody had to be on the baby's side! They all made it so easy, Merle! So easy to get rid of it, as if it was a minor inconvenience. But I knew what they were thinking...'

'There you go again!' Merle said.

'Well I *did* know!' Bev's voice rose. 'Just another Black child. We don't want any more of those, do we?' *Somebody* had to be on the baby's side.'

'And who was on your side?' Merle asked.

'You were, I thought,' Bev said bitterly, and began to struggle off the bed.

'I was,' Merle said, pushing her gently back, 'and I still am. What I think doesn't matter. I told you before: It's your decision, and I accept it.'

'But I'll never know what you really think, will I?' Bev said wistfully.

'We only ever know what people say, Bev,' Merle smiled at her. 'We make up the rest to suit ourselves.'

'Well, I didn't like what they were saying,' Bev admitted, sitting there with her hands clasped round her belly. 'So I said: No! – To all of them. The doctors, my father, and Errol.'

She reached for her mug, and held it out to Merle, smiling. Merle chinked her mug against Bev's, her smile crinkling the laughter lines around her eyes as they both drank.

*F*ireflies

Yesterday I met a man on a train. Two months ago, he told me, his only daughter had taken the elevator up to the top of a tall building in Japan. She was holding a firework in her hand. A Roman candle. She had struck a match and lit the touch-paper, then she had raised the firework high above her head like a torch. It had started to crackle and splutter. Broken lines of white heat had shot out into the night sky—thin darts of light being fired into the blackness, just as a snake might flick out its tongue. Then a fountain of stars had showered down over her head and into her hair, drenching her in brightness. And then she had jumped. She and the firework hit the pavement together, both of them extinguished in the same split second. The rescue workers clearing up afterwards complained very bitterly about the mess.

'They sent us a photograph,' he said emptily. 'But it wasn't the same. It could have been anyone. So then we asked to have the body flown home. And they said that would cost fourteen thousand pounds. We couldn't believe it at first. Fourteen *thousand*! It seemed so incredible. But there was nothing we could do, of course. So we just had to let them cremate her.' He half-smiled, 'Did you know that there are seven different grades of cremation in Japan? They all cost different amounts of money.' I shook my head and said nothing. I didn't trust myself to speak.

'It cost seven hundred pounds,' he continued. 'That was the cheapest. And then I went through to Heathrow to pick up the ashes. They were in a metal urn. And the metal urn itself was in a polythene container that said Human Remains. The taxi-driver gave me a queer look. 'What you got in there mister', he said. 'A dead dog? When I got home I took the urn up to her bedroom, and we didn't open it for two weeks. And all the time in between, I just couldn't stop thinking about her. Wondering why she did it. Wondering if it hurt. Imagining her falling over and over again, that firework in her hand like a shooting star...'

I saw that he was crying quietly.

'In the end, we went upstairs and lit a candle in the room and said a sort of prayer, and took her down from the shelf. There was a plaque screwed down on the outside. Her date of birth, and the date she died. Only they'd got the first date wrong. They put 1960. But really she was just twenty-five. Then we lifted the lid and looked inside. It seemed so easy at first. It was as if it wasn't really her. Just ash and bits of flaky stuff. But then my wife saw something glittering, and put her hand in and lifted it out. It was the steel plate she had put in her knee after the biking accident. That was all there was left of her.'

I didn't know what to say. There we were, in a tin box in the middle of nowhere. I looked at our reflections in the window. Two ghostly heads—facing each other, yet always apart—fixed by the glass in a strange limbo that was neither inside nor out of the train. 'I'm so sorry,' I said hopelessly.

When I got home, Annie and Sophie were in the kitchen making a cake. Annie's my wife. Sophie's our daughter. They had their backs to me, and didn't hear me come in at first as the radio was playing. Sophie was singing along cheerfully. She's the only person I've ever met who knows the lyrics to all the records they play on the radio. Annie says it's because she's watched 'Top of the Pops' every week, almost since it first started. And, not being able to read, she's developed a much better memory than most people. 'Not for tunes she hasn't,' I always say. Sophie's got easily the worst singing voice I've ever heard in my life. When she was little I used to drive her wild playing 'Guess the Song' with her. 'Jingle bells, jingle bells...' she would croak tunelessly. I would frown, and pretend to be thinking really hard. 'Just give me a minute,' I'd say. 'Wait. Yes. It's coming. I've got. it. Away in a Manger!' And she would scream with delight.

'Hey there, growler,' I said as I came in. 'What's cooking?'

Annie explained. 'It's Raymond's twenty-first birthday tomorrow. They're having a party at the Unit.' The Unit is where Sophie and her friends go every day during the week. They do piece-work, sub-contracted out by the larger factories. Until recently they were stamping out the circular pats of butter that go with frozen kippers. But for the last few months they've been working on home-made beer kits. They have to weigh out the hops (none of them can read, so they do that with a system of coloured buckets) and then put them into cardboard boxes. They work from nine until four. Sophie comes back each evening smelling like a brewery, with hops in her nails and her hair and her pockets. Annie always goes straight upstairs to run her a bath. Then on Friday nights there's a special ritual, because that's when she gives us her pay packet and feels very important. She earns £5.50 a week.

'So you're going to take Raymond a cake are you, Sophie?' I said.

Sophie nodded eagerly, and pointed to a box of Smarties.

'When the icing's dry,' said Annie, 'we're going to write his name on the top in green and yellow Smarties. Sophie's already chosen the colours.'

'Terrific,' I said. 'That means I can eat the orange ones.'

Sophie promptly squealed into fits of giggles. She's got quite a sense of humour, has Sophie. She's really quick. In fact, one of the main reasons I wish she could talk is that I just know she would tell very good jokes. But talking is beyond her. Memorising songs is one thing. Finding the words to make a sentence all of her own is something else. No matter how hard she struggles, she simply can't make language work for her.

She adores words, that's the sad thing. She knows that they have magic. Her books, for instance, are her pride and joy—her private treasure chest. She hoards them like a miser. Yet somehow the key is lost to her completely. And every night, at a certain time, her eyes beg silently for either Annie or me to unlock the mystery for her, and read her a story. Sometimes, when she thinks no one's looking, I see her pouring desperately over a printed page, willing it to yield her its secrets. Then I watch her face screw up in frustration, and I wish I could die. And I wonder, all over again, about the strange darkness of her world. What it is that is missing. Why it is that words, for her, are as fascinating but as elusive as fireflies.

Sophie watched, hypnotised, as Annie traced RAYMOND into the butter icing with the tip of a knife. 'Go on then, Sophie,' she smiled, handing her the Smartie box. 'You finish it.' And, too-large tongue clamped between her teeth in familiar attitude of deepest concentration, our daughter carefully laid the green and yellow Smarties along the guidelines, bringing each letter to colourful life with all the reverence and ceremony of a priestess.

Much later, when the cake had been wrapped in cellophane and put into a large square biscuit tin, and when Annie had sewn a button onto Sophie's best blue dress ready for the party, and when I had crept quietly out of Sophie's room, leaving her snoring peacefully, her copy of *Jack and the Beanstalk* still beside her on the bed, I remembered the man on the train. I went to the door and looked out at the night sky. High above me, I saw the tail lights of an aeroplane winking far away into the distance. And I wondered where it was going, and I thought of Japan. Then I pictured a girl—thousands of miles and a life-time away—who had blazed a trail of her own through the darkness, and made fire come out of the sky.

I turned out the light in the hallway. The moonlight spilled like water down the wall.

I had a strange dream during the night. I dreamed about fireflies. I dreamed that it was summer, and that Annie and Sophie and I were on a long white beach somewhere far away. It was eveningtime. But it was still so hot that the sand was

99

warm beneath our feet, and a greenish haze was gleaming above the water. The beach was deserted, I remember, and we were sitting together, the three of us, underneath a curious tree that spread a shadow over the sand. The air was hung with a deep exotic perfume that I couldn't identify, and I remember feeling wonderful. I was drinking a can of beer—much to Sophie's disapproval: she can't understand how anyone could possibly want anything to do with the stuff. And Annie was reading *Robinson Crusoe* aloud. Sophie was spellbound. It's a story she's known for years and years now, but it never fails to thrill her.

Then Annie came to Crusoe's discovery in the cave. '*I saw two broad shining eyes belonging to some creature,*' she read, '*whether devil or man I knew not. They twinkled like two stars.*' I looked at Sophie. Her eyes were shining with excitement. Annie continued, '*But I knew that there could be nothing in this cave that was more frightful than myself; so, plucking up my courage, I took up a great firebrand, and in I rushed again, with a stick flaming in my hand.*' Sophie was staring intently at Annie's face. Her fists were clenched tightly as she waited, rapt, to see whether Crusoe would still escape with his life—or whether this time there might be a disaster. For her each visit to the cave is an entirely new experience.

Very slowly, Annie read on, '*Encouraging myself a little by considering that the power and presence of God was everywhere, and was able to protect me, I stepped forward again.*' Sophie's mouth was wide open. '*And by the light of the firebrand, holding it a little over my head, I saw lying on the ground a most monstrous, frightful old he-goat...*' There was then a squeal of the most absolute joy from Sophie. The whole of the night air echoed with the purity of her laughter. Even the sea seemed to ripple with it. 'And that's all we've got time for this evening,' said Annie.

We gathered up our bits and pieces from under the tree, and began to walk home along the beach. Then, looking out over the water as we walked, I saw that the strange greenish haze was not heat haze at all. It was fireflies. Hundreds of them. A pageant of them. All united in some strange and wonderful magic dance above the emerald water.

I awoke from my dream to the sound of loud splashing noises from the bathroom. Sophie was having her bath. Getting Sophie up and dressed in the mornings takes quite a long time. She has unusually sensitive skin that has to be washed very gently with a special liquid soap. Ordinary soap brings her out in a rash. And she has a bad eye condition. Her eyelids gum together during the night, so she can't see at all when she first wakes up. Her eyes have to be bathed carefully in warm water, and then treated with an ointment. All in all, it generally takes about two hours. She hates to be hurried. So Annie and I have a routine, each of us getting up at six on alternate mornings, to help get her ready for the Unit. This morning was Annie's turn.

I lay thinking about the dream for a little while. The memory of it was still glowing inside me like a light bulb. I remembered the warmth and power of Annie's voice, reading a passage that I've heard her read so often. I remembered the joyful peal of Sophie's laughter. And, as though it were real, I remembered the glory of the fireflies and the luminous trail of phosphorescence that had floated over the waves. I felt overwhelmingly happy and serene. Yet still I was haunted by another vision. The vision of a girl in Japan with a firework in her hand. And I couldn't understand why.

Then I caught sight of the time, and hurried downstairs to fix breakfast. As I passed the bathroom, I saw a familiar pool of water spreading out beneath the door and onto the landing, and I grinned to myself. Sophie was up to her usual tricks. She always insists on filling the bath almost to the brim. Then she sits on the edge and launches herself into it feet first, like a small tanker on a slipway. Sophie's not very tall, but she's very round and heavy. So there's always a massive displacement of bathwater that surges up and over the sides, and floods the floor. We gave up having carpet in the bathroom ages ago. Annie says it's like having a playful pet whale in the house.

Annie is, quite simply, the nicest person I know. Perhaps everyone thinks that about their lover. But in Annie's case it's literally true. Her patience with Sophie is infinite. No matter how long something takes—whatever it is—she's always there as a support. Watching, waiting, and—if Sophie wants her to—helping. I don't think I've ever once seen her get angry or bad-tempered with her. Annie's no saint. She smokes and drinks. She cheats at cards. She swears if she hits her thumb with a hammer. But hers is a very rare form of courage. Because it's courage both for herself and for others. Three weeks after Sophie was born, when they told us what was different about her, Annie locked herself in the bedroom and cried for two days. She couldn't talk to anyone—not even me. I used to leave trays of food outside the door for her. 'I'll come out when I'm ready,' was all she said. And that was the truth. By the time she did come out—pale and needlessly apologetic for the worry she'd caused—she had understood, far better than I ever did, how life was going to be from then on. And she was ready for it.

Annie's a torch-bearer all right. That bit of my dream made some sense. But the dance of the fireflies—and everything else—was still as much of a puzzle to me as ever, as I slopped milk into a jug and hunted frantically for the new packet of cornflakes.

'Sophie's on her way down,' shouted Annie from upstairs. 'Can you do her hair while I look for a birthday card?' And in came Sophie, holding two pieces of velvet ribbon. She looked gorgeous, she really did. I wolf-whistled my approval of the best blue dress, and she gave me a very grown-up smile and blushed bright pink. I felt terribly proud of her. Then she settled down happily on her favourite stool, and I set about plaiting her hair. Sophie has lovely hair. It's very soft and fine, almost like a baby's.

'Will there be lots of people at the party, Sophie?' I asked. She nodded, and waved both her hands around. That meant everybody. I've got pretty good at reading Sophie's sign language. 'And what will you all be singing?' I asked. She beamed. No further invitation was needed. 'Happy birthday to you, happy birthday to you,' she started yelling at the top of her voice, tone-deaf as ever. 'Oh, really?' I said wickedly. 'Ten Green Bottles? Isn't that a bit unusual for a birthday party?'

Annie appeared with a birthday card. 'I'll write your name on it for you, Sophie,' she said, reaching across the table for

Sophie's tin of crayons. Sophie and I both looked at the picture rather doubtfully. 'Sorry it's a bit twee,' said Annie. The picture showed two fluffy kittens popping their heads out of a wicker basket, and the message said 'Have a real cute day!'

'Never mind,' I said consolingly. 'I'm sure the dog'll appreciate it. He'll probably eat it for supper.' Raymond's family pet is only just this side of a wolf.

LOVE FROM SOPHIE, Annie wrote neatly, underneath the sloppy verse wishing Raymond a purr-fect birthday. Sophie watched closely, solemnly at first and then smiling in recognition as Annie read out the words to her. Then, as though something had suddenly occurred to her, she reached for the crayons herself and began to scribble a private design all of her own across the envelope. Completely absorbed in what she was doing, her head bent over the paper, she devised an elaborate pattern of mysterious symbols, using first one colour and then another. I looked on in some amusement. It was like watching someone engaged in a fascinating but wholly incomprehensible board game.

Then came a shrill hooting noise from outside the house. The minibus had already arrived to collect Sophie and take her to the Unit. It was parked in the lane, down by the gate. The bus windows were all misted up, where eager noses were pressed against the glass, but we could still make out the faces of her friends urging her to hurry. Sophie dashed to the door, and Annie and I hurled ourselves madly round the room— gathering up all the things that she'd need for the day and cramming them into her tartan holdall. It was quite a collection. Her form about the outing to the Adventure Centre. Her soap and towel. Her emergency money. A tube of eye-cream. Her new make-up bag. A spare pair of knickers. And—today's special—Raymond's Smartie cake, packed neatly away in its tin. After that, there was time only for one quick kiss for each of us and then she was gone. She rushed off down the garden path and out into the murky October morning.

The house fell silent. Annie poured us both some coffee and we sat quietly together at the kitchen table, recovering our energy. We didn't talk for a while. Annie was reading something very intently. That's her way of unwinding. And I was looking out of the window. It was a dull day. The sky was grey and troubled. And gusts of wind were blowing fitfully, like curls of smoke, scattering ashes from the remains of next door's bonfire across our garden.

The patterns of ash swirled and spun before my eyes. Grey and maddening. Matter without form. And yet again I found myself remembering the man on the train. Why had his story been so important to me? Why had its images burned themselves into my heart? What was it that was whirling faster and faster through my mind now, like flakes of hot ash?

'What's the matter?'

I hear Annie's anxious question as though through a long tunnel. And, then, looking out over the garden, where a squall of wind had begun ripping through the hedgerows, I told her about my dream. And, haltingly, I told her the story of the man on the train.

She said nothing about the dream, and very little about the story. She said only one thing. 'Twenty-five?' she said quietly. 'That's the same age as Sophie.'

I couldn't speak. The most hideous picture had formed in my head. All the familiar things were there. A night sky. A tall building, and a figure at the top of it, waving a lighted firework. Only this time, with a painful effort of will, I forced myself to look closer. And then I saw what I think I'd always half known. The girl with the firework had Sophie's face. I began to shake then, racked by the most dreadful spasms of sickness and guilt. For suddenly it had all become clear to me.

The morning was even darker now. The sky seemed burdened and heavy. The winds and the clouds were gathering force. I could see that it was going to rain at any moment.

'Can I tell you something?' I said slowly.

'Go on,' said Annie.

'The day they first told us about Sophie,' I said, staring blankly out of the window, 'the day you went up to the room and hid away from me. Do you know how I felt then?' Annie didn't speak. Outside the wind was whirling dead leaves from the trees, spinning them through the air, bowling them scornfully down the pathway in crazy drunken cartwheels. 'I sat here,' I said, 'here in this chair, all on my own. Just looking into the fire. Sometimes Sophie would start to cry in the other room. I'd hear her, quite distinctly. But I'd do nothing at all about it. Deliberately. I simply couldn't make myself move. Can you begin to imagine what I was thinking?'

It had finally started to rain. Splashes of water were throwing themselves blindly against the window, smashing into the glass. They shattered like moths on a car windscreen. Then I watched them stream away into nothingness. My vision was blurring. I couldn't look at Annie. 'I wanted her to die,' I said miserably. 'That was all I wanted then in the whole world. Her to die. Then you would come back to me. And everything could be just as it was before.' I couldn't see anything any more. I was staring straight into silence. All the secret shame that had been welling up inside of me for twenty-five years had finally flooded out. At last I'd said it. Yet I felt no relief at all—only utter desolation and wretchedness. 'Can you ever forgive me?' I said.

Neither of us spoke for what felt like a very long time. I could hear my watch ticking. I was standing on the edge of darkness with a lighted firework in my hand. Then, calm and low, came Annie's voice. 'Have you never realised that I was thinking exactly the same thing?' she said softly.

That was all she said. She didn't need to say anything else. A dark shadow was leaving me, like a ghost vanishing at cock-crow. The non-existent firework spun out of my hand into a blackness that was no longer there. And very slowly, with a grave and growing sense of wonder, I became conscious of a light more intense and a stillness more perfect than anything I'd ever known before.

Outside, the wind and the rain were now dying away, and—through window-panes washed clean by the rain-water—I saw that everything was quiet once more in the garden. Only the gate was still moving. It swung open, just as Sophie had left it. And in a few hours' time—to our joy and to hers—she would be rushing back through it again, happy and laughing. A little fat figure with shining eyes—velvet ribbons no doubt unfastened by then, but still bright and beautiful in her very best blue dress. Sophie. Our daughter.

Then I felt Annie pass something to me, across the table.

'What is it?' I said.

It was the envelope that Sophie had been drawing on. In her excitement she had forgotten to take it with her. Annie turned it upside down for me carefully. And it was only then that I saw what had appeared to me at first as scribble, a random collection of coloured shapes, was not scribble after all. The letters were hesitant and shaky, formed with great labour in thick wax crayon by someone who had never written a word before in her whole life. Yet they were completely unmistakeable – seven green and yellow letters arranged in perfect sequence from the R to the D. They were the letters from the top of the birthday cake.

Annie looked at me and smiled. 'It's a firefly,' she said.

LINDA COOKSON

*P*ersonal Essay

I never write stories in the way I was always told to at school. It is really only very rarely, for instance, that I know how a story will end when I first start writing it. Sometimes I might *think* I know. But then suddenly, once I'm actually involved in the writing, that ending will no longer seem right. Instead, something totally different will present itself as the obvious — maybe even the only *possible* way for that story to make sense. That can be a very odd feeling sometimes. I have never been to a seance, but I imagine just how it would feel if the glass were suddenly to shoot away from under your fingertips and take on a momentum of its own. All at once, as you write, you start to feel that the characters have taken over and are creating their own fate.

That, for me, is where things become exciting. I find beginning stories quite difficult — even, sometimes, quite painful. Usually, at the back of my mind there will be one single image — almost like a snapshot — that has made me begin in the first place. In 'Fireflies' it was the vision of a human firework — a girl falling from the sky like a shooting star. But then other images begin to superimpose themselves. Things take me by surprise. I had no idea, for example, that the man telling the story in 'Fireflies' had a handicapped daughter until the moment when he walked through the back door and found her there, icing the cake. But I know that these pictures must be suggesting themselves to me for a reason. So what I have to do then is to make sense of them all. I need to find out what it is that links all of these separate lives and actions together.

In my stories, people often make discoveries — especially about the links between the present and the past, between people and places, between small incidents and large events. It's as though they suddenly hold the kaleidoscope still for a moment, and see the patterns. Or press the 'freeze-frame' on a video. In a way, I suppose that's also what happens to me as I write. I start to see connections that I'd never thought possible. Things start to take on a curious order.

Short stories are much neater in that way than novels, of course. In a short story there *must* be a special shape, a tight logical link that holds everything together. There simply isn't the space to describe characters or happenings that have no direct relevance. In my stories, that link is often something visual. In 'Fireflies' it's the fireflies themselves, I suppose – which link the firework at the beginning with the yellow and green lettering at the end. I try sometimes to make the visual image, suggest a particular idea. Here, the fireflies suggest words. If 'Fireflies' could be said to be 'about' anything, I see it mostly as a story about the need for words.

I don't consciously think of my stories as being 'about' things, though. Oddly enough, most of the time I think of them as being rather like lyric poems – short sequences of thoughts and images centred around a particular focal point. It has always seemed to me that short stories have much more in common with poetry than with novels, partly because of their compactness, and the way in which they're so tightly controlled. Partly, of course, it's because they very often only focus on a single place or moment in time. But it also, I think, has something to do with the very intense *emotional* appeal that a short story can make to the reader – which couldn't possibly be sustained throughout a long novel. And that's quite important to me. When I wrote 'Fireflies', I wanted the story to make the people who read it think about some things that they might not have thought about before. I also wanted them to *feel*.

In its final form, 'Fireflies' is completely fictional. The characters and the main narrative line are all invented. But, like all of my stories to a lesser or greater extent, it grew from several things that have happened in my life. I have a Downs Syndrome brother, for example — so some of the detail about Sophie's work and daily life is drawn from experience. I also really did meet a man on a train, whose daughter had leapt from a high building in Japan (although not with a firework). All of those things find their way at the time into my mental notebook. Sooner or later they re-surface, in the most unpredictable of ways, into my stories. I am not, on the whole, a very imaginative person. I am more of a magpie, I think. I tend to hoard up details of things that have happened to me or to people that I know. But when I finally come to write about them they've always changed in some way. Sometimes out of all recognition.

IAN LUMSDEN

*T*he Scythe

I was seven and my best friend was a man of seventy-four. But we really were best friends. We used to go everywhere together. Except for school. Billy was too old for school.

'I've given up learning, Jim,' he told me once. 'I'm starting to forget now.'

I'd been brought up in the city where we'd lived in a terraced house in a street full of children. Then my dad got it into his head to move into the country as the manager of a little pub in the village of Newton in Cumberland.

It was exciting moving house. We sat on the large front seat of the furniture van with the removal men. My dad had always worked behind a bar but this was to be his first real job as manager and he was as excited as I was. My mam had kept telling him to calm down. 'Act your age,' she'd say and then they'd both explode with laughter for no reason at all. Then my mam would hug me to her and point out the countryside as we drove past. Then my dad would ask the driver for the umpteenth time if we were nearly there yet. And then I'd ask my dad exactly the same thing.

The Cumberland was built from solid stone blocks and was covered in ivy. When we drew up outside, mam let out a sigh of pleasure and my dad said proudly, 'I told you so, didn't I?'

'It's lovely,' she said. 'Lovely, isn't it James?'

It was. And there was all the exploring to do. Every room was an adventure. From my bedroom window at the back I could see the blue waters of the Solway Firth. The bar smelt of beer and tobacco. The cellar was dark and mysterious with huge, swollen barrels of beer. The bottle on the shelves were stamped with colourful labels and lovely names like Nut Brown and Milk Stout. There was a dart board, a snooker table, bar skittles, pictures and trophies. I was mad with excitement and tore from room to room yelling out at each new discovery. Eventually, of course, I got too much for my mam and dad and was told to go out and play.

So I ran out all excited like I'd done every day at our old house. I explored the garden and the out-houses. I chased a chicken out of the gate. And then I looked around for someone to join me, like I'd been used to. But no one did. Not then, nor for all the days it took to dawn on me that there just weren't any other children my own age living in that part of the village.

Newton sprawled for several miles along a backroad to the coast and by our pub there were just a few small cottages and a farm with a smelly manure heap that my mam went mad about.

I did everything I could. I bounced a ball for hours on end in the front car park waiting for someone to see me. I sang songs at the top of my voice for someone to hear me. I spread out my very best toys on a blanket hoping to attract other children and tempt them to play. I became desperate for a friend; I'd even have settled for a girl. My mam and dad tried, I remember, but they were too busy for me, sorting out the house and the pub. I grew tired of exploring. At night I cried in my bed for the children I'd left behind and prayed for a friend to join me.

School didn't help. Each morning I had to get the school bus. Nobody seemed to take any notice of me. They all seemed to have a friend to sit beside already. I'd walk down the aisle of a bus full of strangers. And at school, when the monitor rang the bell and we streamed out into the playground, I was left alone, pretending I had something to do.

There's an old black and white picture of Billy Little glued in one of our photograph albums. He's drinking a pint of beer outside my dad's pub. He's got a cap on and brilliant white hair underneath and although he isn't wearing a tie he's got his shirt buttons done up right to the top. He doesn't look happy at all. Perhaps he'd done his collar up too tightly for the photographer.

I used to see Billy working in the kitchen of the labourer's cottage at the back of our garden. He had to do his own washing up. I had my own private place by this time. It was right at the top of the roof. Our pub used to join on with a disused barn where two of our dog's pups were later to be killed when an old door fell on them. It broke their backs. Dad had used the door to partition a place off so that our dog could nurse her pups. I'd been promised the fawn one with the big eyes. Yes, I remember the barn well. I used to sit on that barn. I used to feel quite daring; I can't understand why my mam let me. But I felt important on top of that barn. And when I looked down I could see Billy looking up at me from his cottage.

I can still see him clearly in my mind's eye. But when I look at the photograph, somehow or other the face doesn't register. I remember the cap and the white hair, but I've forgotten Billy's face. Yet in the golden days of my childhood, I remember Billy and the memory is more clear than that neat, black and white photograph. After all, black and white can't show you the suntan, can it? And I remember Billy was always suntanned.

As clear as yesterday I remember the day we first met. My dad had never had a garden of his own and when we got to the pub we discovered a huge garden with gooseberry bushes, a pear tree and a lawn. One of the locals gave dad a lawnmower and I tried to mow the lawn myself one hot summer's day.

I was pushing and straining, and the grass was clogging up the roller and the blades. I couldn't get it to move or do anything. My dad had a go, pushing it up and down a bit but he quickly tired of it.

'I'll leave it to you, son,' he said and went back inside to stack some bottles on the shelves.

Billy was watching me from his window and he could see me
suffering. I'd never spoken to him before. Dad had told me there
was an old man living behind us who had been very ill. But Billy
didn't look ill. His eyes were twinkling as he carefully climbed
the rickety fence separating our gardens. He stood watching me
struggle for a minute or two, stroked his chin and said, 'You'll do
yourself a mischief pushing that at your age.' He looked con-
temptuously at the lawnmower. 'Did your dad buy this?'

'He was given it by a man.'

He snorted and muttered something I couldn't quite make
out. 'Come on,' he said. 'I'll show you what to do.' He turned
to his cottage.

Suddenly he swung round to face me. 'Wait a second, I'm
forgetting myself. We haven't been introduced, have we? My
name's Billy Little. What's yours?'

'James Simpson,' I said, 'and I'm seven.'

'And I'm seventy-four. Pleased to meet you, Jim.' He held
out his hand. I'd never shaken hands before. It felt grown up.
My hand was lost in his though. His skin was as hard as an old
boxing glove.

Then he winked at me. 'We're friends now, eh?'

And I looked up at him and smiled into his twinkling old
eyes.

He went into the shed at the bottom of his garden and he
brought out a scythe with a sort of ebony, black handle—I can
picture it still. It had a curved, steel blade, sharp as a razor, and
it fairly dazzled you when the sun hit it.

Do you know, the grass was knee-high in places. Full of
flowers and different types of grasses, bursting seed heads.

Billy Little waved me to one side and in one fluid, rhythmic
sweep, he sliced through the grass, really near to the roots. It
takes a good lawnmower to do that. He was like a machine. He
started at one end of the garden and, in no time at all, he was
at the other; easily, without any obvious strain. The whole
garden. My dad saw him and went back in again as soon as he
realised that the grass was being cut.

That was the start of my friendship with Billy Little.

The next morning was the last of the Summer Term and I stood waiting nervously for the school bus in my cap and short trousers. Billy came out of his cottage to see me off. My head was down and I didn't see him at first.

'Keep your pecker up, Jim,' he said. 'Chin up, there's a lad. There's nothing to be feared of.'

'I've no one to sit beside,' I said. 'I hate school.'

'It's only one day, then we've got the whole holiday, haven't we?'

The bus came then. I turned anxiously to Billy but he winked at me. 'I'll see you tonight, eh?'

I clambered in and got a seat at the front on the side nearest Billy. As we moved off he pummelled his chin with his fist. The doors closed and over the roar of the engine I could hear him shout, 'Pecker up, Jim.'

He was retired. I never found out what job he'd done. I suppose, like everyone else in the village, he'd been connected with the farming trade but I can't remember him telling me that, I don't even know whether he was a widower or if he never married. I suppose some others might have asked: 'What was your wife like, Mr Little?...Oh, are you very sad now she's dead, Mr Little? Why didn't you ever get married, Mr Little?' I never asked him anything like that. He was just there. I didn't have what you call great conversations with him. I just remember doing things.

He taught me to swim. The Solway Firth, as I've said, was very near and there was this great big marsh, and although it isn't very picturesque when the tide's out, all greyish sand and seaweed, he taught me to swim there in one of the pools. Not like you get in Cornwall, this was just a grass and mud pool. But he taught me to swim there. He really did. He sat on the side and patiently let me find out how to swim myself while he smoked his pipe. And I did swim! I remember floating. He never got in, or even said much. There was no need to. He just watched me.

He showed me where to get the very best mushrooms—at dawn, on the marsh with seagulls screaming overhead and lapwings stalking the sandbanks in their thousands and the silver, clear light of the early morning when I felt like a king at the birth of the world. Billy, guiding me to the secret spots

114

where the mushrooms sprouted among the marsh grass and the sheep droppings, and me, in my warm, woollen sweater, snapping them off into mam's canvas bag: thick, flabby mushrooms that bulged out of the bag. And then, elated and proud, catching my dad just as he had got up, and tipping the mushrooms into a heap on the kitchen table. And Billy winking at my dad, and later, the three of us, gorged on mushrooms; Billy, my dad and me.

Then there's the time on the moors with the snake, the time I had nightmares about for ages afterwards. We were just pottering around when something slithered through the heather. Quick as a flash, Billy scooped it into the air with the end of his walking stick. It was a snake: all black and brown zig-zags.

Billy's voice was a whisper, 'It's an adder, Jim. If it bites you you're dead!'

It moved towards us like a live electric wire. All of a sudden— whack! Billy had given it a loud, thick crunch on the top of the head. He killed it stone dead. It twitched and twisted a few times, then lay still. I had a chance to examine it and, rather gingerly, touch it and prod it with my finger.

Not that I want you to think that Billy was destructive because he wasn't. I remember once passing the gamekeeper's cottage near the woods. On the fence there were all sorts of animals hanging up, drying and shrivelling on the barbed wire. All sorts of things: magpies, weasels, tiny shrews, moles. Billy shook his head. I was shocked and fascinated all at once. I said, 'What do they do that for? Why do they put those animals there?'

'Well, Jim,' he said, 'him as lives there will tell you it's to frighten them off. I think they're just trophies. Something to show he's doing his job.'

He shook his head again, took out his pipe and started smoking.

Outside the gamekeeper's cottage was the biggest creature I'd seen in the wild. It was a badger. I had just read *Wind in the Willows* and I had a magical, awed respect for badgers. I hadn't realised they were so big. The gamekeeper had shot it. You could see the hole and the blood. A huge great big badger and its yellow teeth, its front teeth, sort of set in a snarl. And the red hole where it had been shot. Horrifying. It was like seeing a dead family pet.

I could see Billy was affected as well. He said, 'When I was a lad I used to know where there was a badger set. I used to watch it at night. Marvellous how playful they are, badgers. They grunt like pigs.'

Now I can't honestly say he ever took me to see badgers, but I remember that one, and I remember the look of disgust on Billy's face.

I didn't tell all the truth earlier. Billy and I did have one conversation. It was about death but I don't think I fully realised that at the time. It was on the one rainy day I remember in all that long summer.

We were sitting under the chestnut tree by the track that ran alongside Billy's cottage. It was the tree that in the autumn was to grow thick with rich, brown chestnuts that no one except me ever picked. It was such a waste. I used to stuff my pockets full of the things and take them to school where in the playground I was soon surrounded by thrusting hands and became the most popular boy around, while the conkers lasted and I had something to give away.

But those days were far off indeed as me and my best friend Billy sheltered from the rain and listened to it pound on the leaves. I felt special, I suppose, protected by the tree with Billy steady and calm beside me, quietly smoking his pipe.

'I'm never going to die!' I suddenly announced to the world for no reason that I knew of then, or now for that matter. The world seemed alive and rich. The tree was an umbrella sheltering us under a waterfall of green and I felt like I did on top of that barn roof.

'No, I'm never going to die,' I said again because Billy was quiet and thoughtful beside me.

'We all die, Jim,' he said.

'No, we'll never die,' I declared confidently, involving Billy in my sense of immortality.

He smiled at that. Perhaps it was a sad smile, I don't know for sure.

'We'll both die when it's our turn. When the Reaper decides it's time.'

'The Reaper?' I asked, instantly curious.

'The Reaper. You've seen my scythe, Jim?'

I nodded.

'Well the Reaper strides about in the clouds up there and looks down and he has a scythe like mine, only it's much sharper, and he cuts off the lifelines of those he thinks are ripe for harvesting.'

'Ripe?' I wanted to know.

'Ready to die, Jim.'

'What's your lifeline?'

'It's invisible. Like your soul. But the Reaper can see it. We've all got a lifeline.'

'And he kills you with a scythe?'

'Like I said, he cuts your lifeline.'

'And he can see all that from up there?'

'The Reaper can see everything, Jim.'

'Is he God?'

'He's nearly God. He dresses in white and has a long beard.' I was perfectly satisfied with that. I knew God dressed in white and had a long beard.

Spread between the lowest branch of the chestnut tree and the hawthorn hedge behind us was a giant spider's web with a fat, black spider poised in the centre. While Billy had been speaking he had quietly opened out the tiny, silver penknife he used to scrape out his pipe and he sliced through an almost invisible strand of silk that anchored the web to the hedge. Amazingly, the web held and the spider stayed put.

'Why does he use the scythe?'

'A farmer uses a scythe to cut the corn when it's ripe.'

Billy's eyes were fastened on the spider's web. The sun's rays were beginning to pierce the thinning rain clouds and drops of water on the web sparkled like jewels. Billy cut another strand. Still the spider was motionless.

'And when you're ripe you die?' I whispered.

The rain stopped altogether. The sun shone. I became aware of the birds singing and from far off the sound of a tractor starting up.

Another strand of the web was cut and the spider scuttled for the safety of the chestnut tree.

'Are you ripe, Billy?' I asked.

He smiled. 'I think the Reaper missed me, Jim. Sometimes you get that, you know, a stalk of wheat left at the edge of the field after the harvest. Mind you, I've hidden that scythe of mine just in case the Reaper needs another one.'

He gave a final decisive swipe with his penknife and the web folded together and drifted downwards to the grass like a parachute.

'I'm not ripe am I, Billy?'

He ruffled my hair and laughed. 'You? You're just a green shoot, Jim.'

I remember the harvest; the golden, gleaming corn and the days that seemed to last for ever; the fieldmice climbing to the tops of the stalks of wheat and frantically trying to catch as many as I could and put them in Billy's cap. It was great. I got about four in his cap at one time. I can still remember the excitement, yelling like an imbecile into the vast, blue sky. And the sun burned down on our heads as the last of the corn was gathered in.

Really, I suppose, measured in weeks I didn't know Billy for that long. Only that one hot summer.

One day I was sitting on top of the roof, looking down as usual, and I saw the curtains in Billy's cottage were closed. And almost matter-of-factly I said to myself, I wonder if Mr Little is dead? I went and asked my dad and he put his hands on my shoulders.

'Yes, son, he's passed away.'

For about three days, people came and went. I watched them all. I'd hardly ever seen anybody else at Billy's cottage before. My dad took me to the funeral and still it didn't register. I remember I was trying to sell tickets for a school raffle to all the mourners. I didn't realise somehow that Billy was under the soil. You're not conscious of death at that age.

About two days after the funeral, for the very first time, I went into Billy's cottage. Loads of people were there, people from all over the village, people I'd never seen before. And there were tables outside the cottage and all his tools were there, laid out in lines, with people picking them up and inspecting them. And in the living room there were numbers on all his possessions: they were auctioning off all Billy's property.

My dad was having a good look around. I said to him, 'Can we buy the scythe?' I could see it lying on the bench in the back garden.

'No, son, it's too old-fashioned.'

'Please, dad.'

'No, son, no. One or two other things we'll buy, but it's a bit old-fashioned is a scythe. We'll get something else. We've got a lawnmower.' Fat lot of good that did for you, I thought.

I ran right over the lawn and climbed the fence, Billy's fence, into our garden, belted into the house, into the back-kitchen, up the stairs two at a time and into my bedroom. I remember madly rummaging through the drawers until I found my piggy bank, stuffed at the bottom. I tipped all my money out, scooped it into my hands and ran back.

I'd be lying if I said I remember bidding for it, I think my dad must have done that, but in my mind's eye I can see myself giving the man all my pennies. And he gave me the scythe. I held it and I could feel where Billy had gripped the handle, almost as if the black wood had been moulded through the years by Billy's hands. The sharp blade didn't frighten me a bit. I knew Billy's scythe wouldn't hurt me. A green shoot was what he'd called me.

I never did cut the grass with the scythe; it was long and heavy and I was only seven. In the spring when a new boy moved into the farm just a few fields away I forgot Billy, and the scythe grew rusty in my dad's outhouse. But now, when I look back all those years ago, it still hurts to think of Billy and his scythe.

Marriage Is A Private Affair

'Have you written to your dad yet?' asked Nene one afternoon as she sat with Nnaemeka in her room at 16 Kasanga Street, Lagos.

'No. I've been thinking about it. I think it's better to tell him when I get home on leave!'

'But why? Your leave is such a long way off yet – six whole weeks. He should be able to be let into our happiness now.'

Nnaemeka was silent for a while, and then began very slowly as if he groped for his words: 'I wish I were sure it would be happiness to him.'

'Of course it must,' replied Nene, a little surprised. 'Why shouldn't it?'

'You have lived in Lagos all your life, and you know very little about people in remote parts of the country.'

'That's what you always say. But I don't believe anybody will be so unlike other people that they will be unhappy when their sons are engaged to marry.'

'Yes. They are most unhappy if the engagement is not arranged by them. In our case it's worse – you are not even an Ibo.'

This was said so seriously and so bluntly that Nene could

not find speech immediately. In the cosmopolitan atmosphere of the city it had always seemed to her something of a joke that a person's tribe could determine whom he married.

At last she said, 'You don't really mean that he will object to your marrying me simply on that account? I had always thought you Ibos were kindly disposed to other people.'

'So we are. But when it comes to marriage, well, it's not quite so simple. And this,' he added 'is not peculiar to the Ibos. If your father were alive and lived in the heart of Ibibio-land he would be exactly like my father.'

'I don't know. But anyway, as your father is so fond of you, I'm sure he will forgive you soon enough. Come on then, be a good boy and send him a nice lovely letter...'

'It would not be wise to break the news to him by writing. A letter will bring it upon him with a shock. I'm quite sure about that.'

'All right, honey, suit yourself. You know your father.'

As Nnaemeka walked home that evening he turned over in his mind different ways of overcoming his father's opposition especially now that he had gone and found a girl for him. He had thought of showing his letter to Nene but decided on second thoughts not to, at least for the moment. He read it again when he got home and couldn't help smiling to himself. He remembered Ugoye quite well, an Amazon of a girl who used to beat up all the boys, himself included, on the way to the stream, a complete dunce at school.

'I have found a girl who will suit you admirably – Ugoye Nweke, the eldest daughter of our neighbour, Jacob Nweke. She has a proper Christian upbringing. When she stopped schooling some years ago her father (a man of sound judgement) sent her to live in the house of a pastor where she has received all the training a wife could need. Her Sunday School teacher has told me that she reads her Bible very fluently. I hope we shall begin negotiations when you come home in December.'

On the second evening of his return from Lagos Nnaemeka sat with his father under a cassia tree. This was the old man's retreat where he went to read his Bible when the parching

December sun had set and a fresh, reviving wind blew on the leaves.

'Father,' began Nnaemeke suddenly, 'I have come to ask for forgiveness.'

'Forgiveness? For what, my son?' he asked in amazement.

'It's about this marriage question.'

'Which marriage question?'

'I can't – we must – I mean it is impossible for me to marry Nweke's daughter.'

'Impossible? Why?' asked his father.

'I don't love her.'

'Nobody said you did. Why should you?' he asked.

'Marriage today is different...'

'Look here, my son,' interrupted his father, 'nothing is different. What one looks for in a wife are a good character and a Christian background.'

Nnaemeka saw there was no hope along the present line of argument.

'Moreover,' he said, 'I am engaged to marry another girl who has all of Ugoye's good qualities, and who...'

His father did not believe his ears. 'What did you say?' he asked slowly and disconcertingly.

'She is a good Christian,' his son went on, 'and a teacher in a Girls' School in Lagos.'

'Teacher, did you say? If you consider that a qualification for a good wife I should like to point out to you, Emeka, that no Christian woman should teach. St Paul in his letter to the Corinthians says that women should keep silence.' He rose slowly from his seat and paced forwards and backwards. This was his pet subject, and he condemned vehemently those church leaders who encouraged women to teach in their schools. After he had spent his emotion on a long homily he at last came back to his son's engagement, in a seemingly milder tone.

'Whose daughter is she, anyway?'

'She is Nene Atang.'

'What!' All the mildness gone again. 'Did you say Neneataga, what does that mean?'

'Nene Atang from Calabar. She is the only girl I can marry.'

This was a very rash reply and Nnaemeka expected the storm to burst. But it did not. His father merely walked away into his room. This was most unexpected and perplexed Nnaemeka. His father's silence was infinitely more menacing than a flood of threatening speech. That night the old man did not eat.

When he sent for Nnaemeka a day later he applied all possible ways of dissuasion. But the young man's heart was hardened, and his father eventually gave him up as lost.

'I owe it to you, my son, as a duty to show you what is right and what is wrong. Whoever put this idea into your head might as well have cut your throat. It is Satan's work.' He waved his son away.

'You will change your mind, Father, when you know Nene.'

'I shall never see her,' was the reply. From that night the father scarcely spoke to his son. He did not, however, cease hoping that he would realize how serious was the danger he was heading for. Day and night he put him in his prayers.

Nnaemeka, for his own part, was very deeply affected by his father's grief. But he kept hoping that it would pass away. If it had occurred to him that never in the history of his people had a man married a woman who spoke a different tongue, he might have been less optimistic. 'It has never been heard,' was the verdict of an old man speaking a few weeks later. In that short sentence he spoke for all his people. This man had come with others to commiserate with Okeke when news went round about his son's behaviour. By that time the son had gone back to Lagos.

'It has never been heard,' said the old man again with a sad shake of his head.

'What did Our Lord say?' asked another gentleman. 'Sons shall rise against their Fathers; it is there in the Holy Book.'

'It is the beginning of the end,' said another.

The discussion thus tending to become theological, Madubogwu, a highly practical man, brought it down once more to the ordinary level.

'Have you thought of consulting a native doctor about your son?' he asked Nnaemeka's father.

'He isn't sick,' was the reply.

'What is he then? The boy's mind is diseased and only a

123

good herbalist can bring him back to his right senses. The medicine he requires is *Amalile*, the same that women apply with success to recapture their husbands' straying affection.'

'Madubogwu is right,' said another gentleman. 'This thing calls for medicine.'

'I shall not call in a native doctor.' Nnaemeka's father was known to be obstinately ahead of his more superstitious neighbours in these matters. 'I will not be another Mrs Ochuba. If my son wants to kill himself let him do it with his own hands. It is not for me to help him.'

'But it was her fault,' said Madubogwu. 'She ought to have gone to an honest herbalist. She was a clever woman, nevertheless.'

'She was a wicked murderess,' said Jonathan who rarely argued with his neighbours because, he often said, they were incapable of reasoning. 'The medicine was prepared for her husband, it was his name they called in its preparation and I am sure it would have been perfectly beneficial to him. It was wicked to put it into the herbalist's food, and say you were only trying it out.'

Six months later, Nnaemeka was showing his young wife a short letter from his father:

'It amazes me that you could be so unfeeling as to send me your wedding picture. I would have sent it back. But on further thought I decided just to cut off your wife and send it back to you because I have nothing to do with her. How I wish that I had nothing to do with you either.'

When Nene read through this letter and looked at the mutilated picture her eyes filled with tears, and she began to sob.

'Don't cry, my darling,' said her husband. 'He is essentially good-natured and will one day look more kindly on our marriage.' But years passed and that one day did not come.

For eight years, Okeke would have nothing to do with his son, Nnaemeka. Only three times (when Nnaemeka asked to come home and spend his leave) did he write to him.

'I can't have you in my house,' he replied on one occasion. 'It can be of no interest to me where or how you spend your leave – or your life, for that matter.'

The prejudice against Nnaemeka's marriage was not confined to his little village. In Lagos, especially among his people who worked there, it showed itself in a different way. Their women, when they met at their village meeting, were not hostile to Nene. Rather, they paid her such excessive deference as to make her feel she was not one of them. But as time went on, Nene gradually broke through some of this prejudice and even began to make friends among them. Slowly and grudgingly they began to admit that she kept her home much better than most of them.

The story eventually got to the village in the heart of the Ibo country that Nnaemeka and his young wife were a most happy couple. But his father was one of the few people in the village who knew nothing about this. He always displayed so much temper whenever his son's name was mentioned that everyone avoided it in his presence. By a tremendous effort of will he had succeeded in pushing his son to the back of his mind. The strain had nearly killed him but he had persevered, and won.

Then one day he received a letter from Nene, and in spite of himself he began to glance through it perfunctorily until all of a sudden the expression on his face changed and he began to read more carefully.

'...Our two sons, from the day they learnt that they have a grandfather, have insisted on being taken to him. I find it impossible to tell them that you will not see them. I implore you to allow Nnaemeka to bring them home for a short time during his leave next month. I shall remain here in Lagos...'

The old man at once felt the resolution he had built up over so many years falling in. He was telling himself that he must not give in. He tried to steel his heart against all emotional appeals. It was a re-enactment of that other struggle. He leaned against a window and looked out. The sky was overcast with heavy black clouds and a high wind began to blow filling the air with dust and dry leaves. It was one of those rare occasions when even Nature takes a hand in a human fight. Very soon it began to rain, the first rain in the year. It came down in large sharp drops and was accompanied by the lightning and thunder which mark a change of season. Okeke was trying hard not to think of his two grandsons. But he knew he was now fighting a losing battle. He tried to hum a favourite hymn but the pattering of large rain drops on the roof broke up the tune. His mind immediately returned to the children. How could he shut his door against them? By a curious mental process he imagined them standing, sad and forsaken under the harsh angry weather – shut out from his house.

That night he hardly slept, from remorse – and a vague fear that he might die without making it up to them.

Three Dreams In A Desert

Under A Mimosa-Tree

As I travelled across an African plain the sun shone down hotly. Then I drew my horse up under a mimosa-tree, and I took the saddle from him and left him to feed among the parched bushes. And all to right and to left stretched the brown earth. And I sat down under the tree, because the heat beat fiercely, and all along the horizon the air throbbed. And after a while a heavy drowsiness came over me, and I laid my head down against my saddle, and I fell asleep there. And, in my sleep, I had a curious dream.

I thought I stood on the border of a great desert, and the sand blew about everywhere. And I thought I saw two great figures like beasts of burden of the desert, and one lay upon the sand with its neck stretched out, and one stood by it. And I looked curiously at the one that lay upon the ground, for it had a great burden on its back, and the sand was thick about it, so that it seemed to have piled over it for centuries.

And I looked very curiously at it. And there stood one beside me watching. And I said to him, 'What is this huge creature who lies here on the sand?'

And he said, 'This is woman; she that bears men in her body.'

And I said, 'Why does she lie here motionless with the sand pile round her?'

And he answered, 'Listen, I will tell you! Ages and ages long she has lain here, and the wind has blown over her. The oldest, oldest, oldest man living has never seen her move: the oldest, oldest book records that she lay here then, as she lies here now, with the sand about her. But listen! Older than the oldest book, older than the oldest recorded memory of man, on the Rocks of Language, on the hard-baked clay of Ancient Customs, now crumbling to decay, are found the marks of her footsteps! Side by side with his who stands beside her you may trace them; and you know that she who now lies there once wandered free over the rocks with him.'

And I said, 'Why does she lie there now?'

And he said, 'I take it, ages ago the Age-of-dominion-of-muscular-force found her, and when she stooped low to give suck to her young, and her back was broad, he put his burden of subjection on to it, and tied it on with the broad band of Inevitable Necessity. Then she looked at the earth and the sky, and knew there was no hope for her; and she lay down on the sand with the burden she could not loosen. Ever since she has lain here. And the ages have come, and the ages have gone, but the band of Inevitable Necessity has not been cut.'

And I looked and saw in her eyes the terrible patience of the centuries; the ground was wet with tears, and her nostrils blew up the sand.

And I said, 'Has she ever tried to move?'

And he said, 'Sometimes a limb has quivered. But she is wise; she knows she cannot rise with the burden on her.'

And I said, 'Why does not he who stands by her leave her and go on?'

And he said, 'He cannot. Look...'

And I saw a broad band passing along the ground from one to the other, and it bound them together.

He said, 'While she lies there he must stand and look across the desert.'

And I said, 'Does he know why he cannot move?'

And he said, 'No.'

And I heard a sound of something cracking, and I looked,

and I saw the band that bound the burden on to her back broken asunder; and the burden rolled on to the ground.

And I said, 'What is this?'

And he said, 'The Age-of-muscular-force is dead. The Age-of-nervous-force has killed him with the knife he holds in his hand; and silently and invisibly he has crept up to the woman, and with that knife of Mechanical Invention he has cut the band that bound the burden to her back. The Inevitable Necessity is broken. She might rise now.'

And I saw that she still lay motionless on the sand, with her eyes open and her neck stretched out. And she seemed to look for something on the far-off border of the desert that never came. And I wondered if she were awake or asleep. And as I looked her body quivered, and a light came into her eyes, like when a sunbeam breaks into a dark room.

I said, 'What is it?'

He whispered 'Hush! the thought has come to her, 'Might I not rise?' '

And I looked. And she raised her head from the sand, and I saw the dent where her neck had lain so long. And she looked at the earth, and she looked at the sky, and she looked at him who stood by her: but he looked out across the desert.

And I saw her body quiver; and she pressed her front knees to the earth, and veins stood out; and I cried, 'She is going to rise!'

But only her sides heaved, and she lay still where she was.

But her head she held up; she did not lay it down again. And he beside me said, 'She is very weak. See, her legs have been crushed under her so long.'

And I saw the creature struggle: and the drops stood out on her.

And I said, 'Surely he who stands beside her will help her?'

And he beside me answered, 'He cannot help her: *she must help herself*. Let her struggle till she is strong.'

And I cried, 'At least he will not hinder her! See, he moves farther from her, and tightens the cord between them, and he drags her down.'

And he answered, 'He does not understand. When she moves she draws the band that binds them, and hurts him, and he moves farther from her. The day will come when he will understand, and will know what she is doing. Let her once stagger on to her knees. In that day he will stand close to her, and look into her eyes with sympathy.'

And she stretched her neck, and the drops fell from her. And the creature rose an inch from the earth and sank back.

And I cried, 'Oh, she is too weak! she cannot walk! The long years have taken all her strength from her. Can she never move?'

And he answered me, 'See the light in her eyes!'

And slowly the creature staggered on to its knees.

And I awoke: and all to the east and to the west stretched the barren earth, with the dry bushes on it. The ants ran up and down in the red sand, and the heat beat fiercely. I looked up through the thin branches of the tree at the blue sky overhead. I stretched myself, and I mused over the dream I had had. And I fell asleep again, with my head on my saddle. And in the fierce heat I had another dream.

I saw a desert and I saw a woman coming out of it. And she came to the bank of a dark river; and the bank was steep and high. And on it an old man met her, who had a long white beard; and a stick that curled was in his hand, and on it was written Reason. And he asked her what she wanted; and she said 'I am woman; and I am seeking for the land of Freedom.'

And he said, 'It is before you.'

And she said, 'I see nothing before me but a dark flowing river, and a bank steep and high, and cuttings here and there with heavy sand in them.'

And he said, 'And beyond that?'

She said, 'I see nothing, but sometimes, when I shade my eyes with my hand, I think I see on the further bank trees and hills, and the sun shining on them!'

He said, 'That is the Land of Freedom.'

She said, 'How am I to get there?'

He said, 'There is one way, and one only. Down the banks of Labour, through the water of Suffering. There is no other.'

She said, 'Is there no bridge?'

He answered, 'None.'

She said, 'Is the water deep?'

He said, 'Deep.'

She said, 'Is the floor worn?'

He said, 'It is. Your foot may slip at any time, and you may be lost.'

She said, 'Have any crossed already?'

He said, 'Some have *tried!*'

She said, 'Is there a track to show where the best fording is?'

He said, 'It has to be made.'

She shaded her eyes with her hand; and she said, 'I will go.'

And he said, 'You must take off the clothes you wore in the desert: they are dragged down by them who go into the water so clothed.'

And she threw from her gladly the mantle of Ancient-received-opinions she wore, for it was worn full of holes. And she took the girdle from her waist that she had treasured so long, and the moths flew out of it in a cloud. And he said, 'Take the shoes of dependence off your feet.'

And she stood there naked, but for one white garment that clung close to her.

And he said, 'That you may keep. So they wear clothes in the Land of Freedom. In the water it buoys; it always swims.'

And I saw on its breast was written Truth; and it was white; the sun had not often shone on it; the other clothes had covered it up. And he said, 'Take this stick; hold it fast. In that day when it slips from your hand you are lost. Put it down before you; feel your way: where it cannot find a bottom do not set your foot.'

And she said, 'I am ready; let me go.'

And he said, 'No – but stay; what is that – in your breast?'

She was silent.

He said, 'Open it, and let me see.'

And she opened it. And against her breast was a tiny thing, who drank from it, and the yellow curls above his forehead pressed against it; and his knees were drawn up to her, and he held her breast fast with his hands.

And Reason said, 'Who is he, and what is he doing here?'

And she said, 'See his little wings...'

And Reason said, 'Put him down.'

And she said, 'He is asleep, and he is drinking! I will carry him to the Land of Freedom. He has been a child so long, so long, I have carried him. In the Land of Freedom he will be a man. We will walk together there, and his great white wings will overshadow me. He has lisped one word only to me in the desert – 'Passion!' I have dreamed he might learn to say 'Friendship' in that land.'

And Reason said, 'Put him down!'

And she said, 'I will carry him so – with one arm, and with the other I will fight the water.'

He said, 'Lay him down on the ground. When you are in the water you will forget to fight, you will think of him. Lay him down.' He said, 'He will not die. When he finds you have left him alone he will open his wings and fly. He will be in the Land of Freedom before you. Those who reach the Land of Freedom, the first hand they see stretching down the bank to help them shall be Love's. He will be a man then, not a child. In your breast he cannot thrive; put him down that he may grow.'

And she took her bosom from his mouth, and he bit her, so that the blood ran down on to the ground. And she laid him down on the earth; and she covered her wound. And she bent and stroked his wings. And I saw the hair on her forehead turned white as snow, and she had changed from youth to age.

And she stood far off on the bank of river. And she said, 'For what do I go to this far land which no one has ever reached? *Oh, I am alone! I am utterly alone!*'

And Reason, that old man, said to her, 'Silence! what do you hear?'

And she listened intently, and she said, 'I hear a sound of feet, a thousand times ten thousand and thousands of thousands, and they beat this way!'

He said, 'They are the feet of those that shall follow you. Lead on! Make a track to the water's edge! Where you stand now, the ground will be beaten flat by ten thousand feet.' And he said, 'Have you seen the locusts and how they cross a stream? First one comes down to the water-edge, and it is swept away, and then another comes and then another, and then another, and at last with their bodies piled up a bridge is built and the rest pass over.'

She said, 'And, of those that come first, some are swept away, and are heard of no more; their bodies do not even build the bridge?'

'And are swept away, and are heard of no more – and what of that?' he said.

'And what of that...' she said.

'They make a track to the water's edge.'

'They make a track to the water's edge...' And she said, 'Over that bridge which shall be built with our bodies, who will pass?'

He said, '*The entire human race.*'

And the woman grasped her staff.

And I saw her turn down that dark path to the river.

And I awoke; and all about me was the yellow afternoon light: the sinking sun lit up the fingers of the milk bushes; and my horse stood by me quietly feeding. And I turned on my side, and I watched the ants run by thousands in red sand. I thought I would go on my way now – the afternoon was cooler. Then a drowsiness crept over me again, and I laid back my head and fell asleep.

And I dreamed a dream.

I dreamed I saw a land. And on the hills walked brave women and brave men, hand in hand. And they looked into each other's eyes, and they were not afraid.

And I saw the women also hold each other's hands.

And I said to him beside me, 'What place is this?'

And he said, 'This is heaven.'

And I said, 'Where is it?'

And he answered, 'On earth.'

And I said, 'When shall these things be?'

And he answered, '*In the Future.*'

And I awoke, and all about me the sunset light; and on the low hills the sun lay, and a delicious coolness had crept over everything; and the ants were going slowly home. And I walked towards my horse, who stood quietly feeding. Then the sun passed down behind the hills; but I knew that the next day he would arise again.

FOLLOW ON

GENERAL ACTIVITIES

Before Reading

● Read an extract, poem, play or short story which:
 — takes up similar themes or issues
 — presents characters/settings in similar/contrasting ways
 — is written in a similar/contrasting style or genre.

● Take some general issues or questions raised in the story and discuss them in advance to find out how much you and others know and what opinions you have about them. After reading the story, discuss how far your ideas and opinions may have changed.

● Use the titles and/or the first few paragraphs to speculate and predict what the story may be about.

● Take some quotations from the story and speculate how the story will develop.

During Reading

● Stop at various points during reading, and review what has happened so far, then predict what might happen next or how the story may develop.

● Stop at various points and discuss why writers have made certain decisions and what alternatives were open to them.

● Decide who is telling or speaking the story.

● Look out for important quotations that help reveal the meaning of the story.

● Makes notes and observations on plot, character, relationships between characters, style and the way the narrative works.

● Consider the various issues, themes or questions relating to the story which you discussed before reading.

● Build up a visual picture of the setting in order to work out its significance in the story or to represent it as a diagram.

After Reading

● Discuss a number of statements about the story and decide which best conveys what the story is about.

● Prepare a dramatic reading of parts of the text.

● Use the story as a stimulus for personal and imaginative writing:
  — writing stories/plays/poems on a similar theme
  — writing stories/plays/poems in a similar style, genre or with a similar structure

● Discuss and write imaginative reconstructions or extensions of the text:
  — rewriting the story from another character's point of view
  — writing a scene which occurs before the story begins
  — continuing beyond the end of the story
  — writing an alternative ending
  — changing the narrative from the first to the third-person and vice versa
  — experimenting with style and form
  — picking a point in the story where the action takes a turn in direction and rewriting the rest of the story in a different way.

● Represent some of the ideas, issues and themes in the story for a particular purpose and audience:
  — enacting a public inquiry or tribunal
  — conducting an interview for TV or radio
  — writing a newspaper report or press release
  — writing a letter to a specified person or organisation
  — giving an eye-witness report.

● Select passages from the story for film or radio scripting; act out the rehearsed script for a live audience, audio or video taping.

● Write critically or discursively about the story, or comparing one or more story, focusing on:
  — the meaning of the title
  — character, plot and structure
  — style, tone, use of dialect, language
  — build up of tension, use of climax, humour, pathos, etc.
  — endings
  — themes and issues.

Three Resolutions To One Kashmiri Encounter

Before Reading

● Look at the author's sub-title. What does this indicate about the possible direction and content of the story?

● What are your 'images' of India and, in particular, of the Himalayas? Discuss in pairs or groups which films or books have contributed to these images.

● Think of an occasion when you have been approached by a stranger and asked questions. What were your thoughts and reactions? How did the 'encounter' develop? Looking back on the incident do you have any reflections on the way you behaved? Talk about these in groups or improvise one of the incidents.

During Reading

● In his personal essay, Giles Gordon writes of 'the anxiety, the fear, the guilt, the angst in the narrator's mind' (page 10). Trace where these feelings surface in the story as you are reading.

● Pause after the words, 'This head lowered a little in the direction of the ground' (page 4). From this point, the writer offers three alternative endings to the story. Discuss what form these might take.

● 'The reader, painlessly, should have a "feel" of the place' (page 11). Make a note of the descriptions of people and places.

After Reading

● The writer presents three different 'solutions'. Which of these did you find the most satisfying as a reader? Which did you feel was the most likely outcome, bearing in mind what we are told about the narrator?

● In what ways have these 'encounters' changed the narrator? Why do you think Giles Gordon chose to write three different conclusions? Re-read his personal essay.

● Rewrite the story from the Indian's viewpoint. Remember to use the first-person ('I') narrative.

● What pictures of the Himalayan area emerge during the narrative? If you were making a short film of this story which particular images would you focus on to help create a clear sense of place and its local people?

● Write your own story set 'in foreign parts'. Try to weave in what Giles Gordon calls 'an element of travelogue, of exoticism, of different climate and culture'.

● Write your own story with three different endings. This could be imaginary, or you could base it on a real experience which ended in one particular way but which, looking back on it, you may have wished could have been resolved slightly differently. Remember to jot down ideas, then draft, then write out a final version carefully checked for spelling, sentence structures and paragraphs.

● 'It is easier, difficult though it is, to conjure fiction than to document fact, I believe, and hope you do that fiction is usually closer to life as we experience it, than to reality' (page 12). Use this quotation as a starting-point for *either* a group debate *or* a piece of controversial writing which includes examples from you own reading of fact and fiction.

● '"The novel" is essentially a nineteenth century form, those wonderful slabs or doorstops of narrative, of tuppence-coloured characters in motion. Today television does, for better or for worse, what the novel did. Fiction has had to find a new purpose' (page 11).

Discuss Giles Gordon's observations in small groups. Do you agree with him? Does television work better than a novel or a short story? From your own reading, what are the *special* features and successes of poetry, plays, short stories or novels? Debate this in an essay.

The Life You Save May Be Your Own

Before Reading

● In what contexts have you seen these words written or heard them quoted? How might they be significant as the title of a short story?

● This story is set in the Southern States of the USA during the 1950s. What images do you have from reading or watching films of the South? Talk about these in groups.

● 'Love' and 'Trust' are two key ingredients in this story. In small groups discuss what these words mean to you. What books have you read in which these key elements of fiction have been imaginatively explored?

During Reading

● Pause after the words, '"what is a man?"' (page 16). What picture do we have of the characters at this point?

● Stop reading after the sentence, 'She was ravenous for a son-in-law' (page 18). In pairs, discuss how you think the rest of the story will develop.

● Stop reading after the sentence, 'He drove very fast because he wanted to make Mobile by nightfall' (page 22). How might the story end?

● Flannery O'Connor establishes her characters and their identity through their physical appearance and through what they *say*. Make a note of the dialogue they share, the *way* they speak to each other and their reactions to one another. How do these prepare the reader for the story's ending?

After Reading

● Comment on the battle of words and wit between Mr Shiftlet and the old woman.

● Decide which of the following statements best sums up the story as a whole. Find examples from the text to back up your conclusion.
— This story is about human happiness
— This story is about mother/daughter relationships
— This story is about deceit and greed
— This story is about human disability
— This story is about ambition.
Are there any other statements you want to add?

● Discuss in groups the significance of the tale about the human heart — see page 15.

● One critic has commented on Flannery O'Connor's stories, 'The physical deformity and material poverty of her characters are intended to function beyond the level of documentary to indicate a more general spiritual deformity, a poverty of the soul not confined to any one geographical region'. Write a review of 'The Life You Save May Be Your Own' which comments on both the 'documentary' aspect of the story and on the more general ideas it contains.

● 'The Life You Save May Be Your Own' was first published as one of 'nine stories about original sin' (Flannery O'Connor's description). The sin is usually some form of vanity or self-love. Each story has a moment of grace, revelation, or retribution. Where retribution occurs, it is often violent, and the character accepts or fails to accept enlightenment about the poverty of his or her existence and the need for personal change and reform.

First　Improvise and act out the main scenes in the story.

Second　Discuss in groups what each character might have learned from their encounters.

Third　Imagine you are one of the three main characters. Write up their memories (perhaps at a few months distance) of the events that took place.

● Write the stories of what happens to young Lucynell and Mr Shiftlet after they part company at 'The Hot Spot'.

● Write you own short story or radio script in which one person convincingly deceives another person.

● The following are quotations from 'The Life You Save May Be Your Own'. Use them – in any order – to write your own narrative:

— 'I'd give a fortune to live where I could see me a sun do that every evening'.

— 'Nothing is like it used to be, lady. The world is almost rotten'.

— 'There's some men that some things mean more to them than money'.

— 'Lady, a man is divided into two parts, body and spirit'.

— 'Break forth and wash the slime from this earth'.

A Drive In The Country

Before Reading

● In pairs talk about what it is that attracts people to one another. This might be attraction in love, hate or friendship.

● In small groups make a list of those things which cause conflict between the different generations. What are your own experiences of conflicting generations?

● Have you ever wished 'to get away from it all'? What course of action have you imagined yourself taking?

During Reading

● Pause after the words, 'He was locking something out...' (page

26). What is this 'something'?

● Stop after the words, 'She stood planning her treachery' (page 26). Predict the next few paragraphs of the story.

● Look out for words and phrases which help establish the identity of each of Graham Greene's characters.

● Make a note of the *style* of writing which helps build suspense as the plot unfolds.

● Stop after the words, 'irresponsibility and a safe love, danger and a secure heart' (page 35). How will the story end? Discuss this question in groups and decide on just *two* alternatives.

After Reading

● You may know the following lyrics from a song by The Beatles:

'Wednesday morning at five o'clock as the day begins
Silently closing her bedroom door
Leaving the note that she hoped would say more
She goes downstairs to the kitchen clutching her handkerchief
Quietly turning the backdoor key
Stepping outside she is free.

She (We gave her most of our lives)
is leaving (Sacrificed most of our lives)
home (We gave her everything money could buy)
She's leaving home after living alone
For so many years. Bye, bye.....'

How do the feelings of the girl in the song compare with those of the girl in the story? Write your own poem which tries to capture a breakdown of love, friendship or understanding.

● What references are there in the story to religion and religious beliefs? What are the attitudes towards religion of the two central characters? You will need to examine the text very closely for clues and ideas.

● Rewrite the story from the girl's viewpoint. This could be done in the form of a series of diary entries or as a letter to her parents.

● Imagine that you are an investigative reporter looking into the death of Fred. Write up your interviews in note form and then draft a final news report, giving a headline which presents an unusual angle on the events.

● The Samaritans organisation exists to help people in distress, particularly those who might at some point feel suicidal. Imagine that Fred telephones the Samaritans for help and you are at the other end of the line. Write a script of the conversation.

● The conclusion of Graham Greene's novel *Brighton Rock* has striking similarities to 'A Drive in the Country'. Read the final chapters of the novel and compare and contrast plot, characters and style.

● This short story would make an excellent television play. Write the script and make a list for the producer and camera people of some key 'shots' to make the drama come alive.

Talks With My Uncle Moro

Before Reading

● Have you known someone around whom there has been a sense of mystery? In pairs, and then small groups, talk about the person and what mysteries were associated with them.

● Who do you talk to when you want to share a 'secret'? Why is it that particular person whom you choose?

● 'Someone who has influenced me'. Use this as a starting-point for small group discussion.

● 'It's a sad thing, but people are never happy until they have got you categorised. If you let them they'll put you in a little box with all your details on the lid — just like some species of moth'. These are words from Uncle Moro in the story – do you agree with them? To what extent can the roots of *prejudice* be traced to this human habit of categorising others?

During Reading

● Make a list of any clues which help unravel the mystery of Uncle Moro's personal history.

● How do the boy's reactions to and understanding of Uncle Moro shift in the course of the story?

● 'Uncle Moro didn't get back the following spring' (page 46). Pause after this sentence. Predict how the story concludes.

After Reading

● Imagine several years have passed after the end of the story and the boy is thinking back to Uncle Moro. Write an interview with the boy in which he shares what he learnt about life and people from Uncle Moro.

● Make a list of the various prejudices that are shown towards Uncle Moro in the course of the tale. What is the basis and nature of each of the prejudices? How would you explain each of them to a young person who has not yet understood what prejudice is?

● Geoffrey Dean employs an easy and personal style of writing. Using a similar style, write two or three additional scenes between Uncle Moro and the boy which could be woven into the narrative and which add to their mutual understanding.

● Write the story of Uncle Moro and 'the young woman with the long hair'.

● Use any of the following as starting-points for your own creative writing – poetry, prose or drama-script:
— The woman with no name
— Remembering past sadness
— A secret uncovered
— Possessions tie you down
— The Great Philosopher.

A Father

Before Reading

● Disagreements and conflicts are a feature of family life. What particular subjects provide a focus for argument in you family? Are there 'special' conflicts and/or understandings between say, fathers and daughters or mothers and sons?

● Do you know anyone who has moved from one country to live in another? Have you read a book or seen a film which focuses on the problems and opportunities of moving from one culture to another? Discuss your thoughts in groups.

● Different cultures have certain fixed ideas about 'femininity' and 'masculinity'. Talk about these in pairs and then in groups.

During Reading

● Look out for clues as to Babli's social attitudes and how these might have been formed.

● Make a note of the way in which the author reveals the attitudes of Mr and Mrs Bhowmick:
  (a) to each other
  (b) to life in Detroit as opposed to life in India

● Make a list of Mr Bhowmick's superstitions.

● Pause after the sentence, 'His brisk, bright engineer daughter was pregnant' (page 55). What action will Mr Bhowmick take?

● Stop after the words, 'His wife had a rolling pin in one hand' (page 59). Predict how you think the story will end. Do this in pairs, in small groups and then as a whole group, deciding on just *two* possible alternatives.

After Reading

● There are several different conflicts at work in this story:
  — father and daughter
  — father and mother
  — religious superstition and everyday realities
  — traditional and contemporary views about the woman's role in marriage
  — traditional and contemporary attitudes towards conception of children.
Which of these do you feel most concern the writer? What 'conclusions' or 'solutions' does she present to the reader? Is there any significance in the title of the story?

● Sum up the range of reactions and feelings from Mr and Mrs Bhowmick towards their daughter's pregnancy. Although they pointedly do not do this in the original story, write an extra scene in which mother and father openly talk about their attitudes to Babli.

● The story is told by a third-person narrator looking from outside at the events in this family, although the author clearly 'loads the dice'. Rewrite the tale from the point of view of *one* of the main characters.
● Imagine you are a police officer trying to find out the full background facts at the end of the story. Write and then act out the

interviews you have in turn with Mr, Mrs and Babli Bhowmick. Use the close detail of the original text to establish the arguments each of the characters is likely to advance.

● Bharati Mukherjee is a contemporary writer, she was born in Calcutta and moved to live in Canada and the USA. The following quotations are taken from an introduction to her work:

> 'In my fiction 'immigrants' were lost souls, put upon and pathetic. Expatriates, on the other hand, knew all too well who and what they were, and what foul fate had befallen them'.

> 'In the years that I spent in Canada — 1966 to 1980 — I discovered that the country is hostile to its citizens who had been born in hot, moist continents like Asia; that the country proudly boasts of its opposition to the whole concept of cultural assimilation. In the Indian immigrant community I saw a family of shared grievances'.

> 'I have joined imaginative forces with an anonymous, driven, underclass of semi-assimilated Indians with sentimental attachments to a distant homeland but no real desire for permanent return'.

> 'I see most of these as stories of broken identities and discarded languages, and the will to bond oneself to a new community, against the ever-present fear of failure and betrayal'.

Think about these observations in relation to 'A Father'. Write a critical review of the story showing how it brings to the surface many of the concerns and themes identified by the author in the above quotations.

Sphinxes

Before Reading

● What is 'prejudice'? Look up the word in a dictionary. Why does it happen? What are its roots and root causes? Discuss these questions in small groups.

● What is 'privacy'? Why is it important to many people? Why do the news media seek to 'invade' some people's private lives?

● Think of an occasion when someone made an unreasonable request of you, or at least one that *you* thought was unreasonable.

Talk about your reactions in pairs and then in small groups.

● What is your reaction to strangers who knock at your front door? Do you start talking with them or turn them away without a word? Make a list of your group's different responses and then share them with the whole group.

During Reading

● Pause after the sentence, 'At eleven-thirty the following morning the girl in blue was standing smiling at Mr Hovsepian's door' (page 67). Predict what happens next.

● Pause again after the words, 'Two hours later the door knocker sounded' (page 70). What follows? Discuss this in pairs, then small groups, then decide as a whole group on *two* possible ways forward for the story.

● Pause at the end of page 80, at the sentence, 'She stopped, a trifle breathless, just in front of him'. How will the story end?

● Make a list of the different names given to Mr Hovsepian by his visitors. What effect does this have?

● Make up a time-chart for the story. Trace how Mr Hovsepian reacts hour by hour as the plot unfolds.

After Reading

● Which of the following do you think prompted the writer to create this unusual story:
   — An interest in showing how prejudice operates
   — A concern for the rights of the individual citizen
   — An attempt to reveal one man's silly objections to a harmless form
   — A wish to criticise the way officials approach their jobs.
Can you think of any other ideas behind this narrative?

● Write a critical review of the story, including commentary on:
   — significance of the title
   — structure and build-up of the narrative
   — relationships between different characters
   — role of Desmond and family
   — humour in the situation
   — how the story ends.

● Rewrite the story from the point of view of the girl in blue. Look back carefully at the text to establish her exact attitude towards Mr Hovsepian.

● The story would make an excellent television or radio script. It could clearly be interpreted in very contrasting ways — for example, either with a strong *comic* approach or with rather *sinister* undertones. Draft out and tape your own script, working in small groups.

● A surprisingly large number of official people and organisations have right of access to your home, apart from a police officer with a warrant! Find out who they are and why they can have access. Debate whether you think these groups *should* be able to enter your home.

● The Official Secrets Act, the Data Protection Act and a possible Freedom Of Information Act are frequently discussed in our society. Find out what you can about these Acts. Do you think you should have access to any records kept on you – for example, school reports, doctors' notes, etc? Hold a group debate in which you bring together the various arguments for and against Freedom of Information.

He Said...

Before Reading

● Think about a time when you have been let down or deceived by someone close to you. In pairs, talk about your feelings as you remember them.

● Do you think women and men react differently to the same situation? Is it possible to characterise male reactions in one way and female reactions in another? Does this just become a form of crude stereotyping? Think of examples and talk about them in groups.

During Reading

● Watch for how Bev changes her feelings and self-image as the story develops. Make a note also of how other characters act towards her.

● Look out for the difference between *male* and *female* reactions to Bev.

● Pause after the sentence, 'I bet he takes longer to decide which *tie* to wear' (page 93). What is Bev's state of mind at this point in the story? Has Merle helped a decision? What will the decision be?

● Stop after the words, 'he smiled as his eyes slipped down over her swollen belly' (page 93). In pairs and then in small groups decide how you feel the story will develop from this point. Try this task in single-sex groupings.

After Reading

● In what way is Barbara Burford openly critical of the men Bev encounters in her life? How does she draw the reader's sympathies away from the men and towards the women in the story? Does the writer *stereotype* to make a point?

● There are several scenes in this story which are mentioned in passing or we assume must have taken place at some point. Improvise one or more of the following:
— the scene in which Errol uses the opening words, 'This is special, so special'....
— the scene in which Bev's father shouts 'My daughter is dead' (page 84)....
— the scene in which Mavis and Bev part company (page 84)....
— a scene in which Bev, thinking to herself or talking further with Merle, makes up her mind to keep the baby — after the break in text on page 93....

Try to keep to the same style as the author.

● Draft and then act out the following scenes which might take place after the baby has been born:
— a chance meeting with Errol and Bev
— a further scene with Merle supporting Bev
— a planned meeting between Bev and her parents
— an interview with her social worker in which Bev talks about her first few months as a single parent

● Use any of the following quotations from the story for *either* a factual piece of writing about an experience of your own, *or* as lines in an imaginary short story or playscript:
— 'I don't know what I'd do in your position. But I would want it to be *my* decision; no one else's'.
— 'Fine gestures are great, in the short run. But you have to live with the consequences for a long time. Is that worth a moment's satisfaction?'
— 'We only ever know what people say. We make up the rest to suit ourselves'.

● The subject of unwanted pregnancies and abortions is a sensitive subject for many people and one that is always being debated by various interest groups. Carry out some research into the views of different groups in society — for example, the Church, the medical profession, the Family Planning Association, politicians, Society for the Protection of Unborn Children, etc. Write up your research and hold a debate in groups on the subject.

Fireflies

Before Reading

● In her Personal Essay Linda Cookson writes, 'I find beginning stories quite difficult…Usually, at the back of my mind there will be one single image that has made me begin in the first place. In 'Fireflies' it was the vision of a human firework' (page 107). In small groups, talk about some possible ingredients for this story.

During Reading

● Pause after the words, 'I'm so sorry', I said hopelessly' (page 97). Put yourself in the position of the narrator — what feelings are you experiencing? How would you respond to the man on the train? How do you think the rest of the story might develop?

● 'In my stories people often make discoveries – especially about the links between the present and the past, between people and places, between small incidents and large events. It's as though they suddenly hold the kaleidoscope still for a moment, and see the patterns. Or press the "freeze-frame" on a video' (page 109). Look out for 'patterns' and 'discoveries' as you are reading.

● Images of light and colour play an important part in both the style and content of 'Fireflies'. Trace these through the text and comment on their usage.

After Reading

● Write a news report of the suicide at the start of the story. Imagine you have interviewed some friends of the girl and some eye-witnesses to piece together a full – and unnerving! – report, with an eye-catching headline.

● A distinctive feature of the author's style is her use of figurative language, for example:

— 'thin darts of light being fired into the blackness, just as a snake might flick out its tongue'.

— 'the moonlight spilled like water down the wall'.

— 'the memory of it was still glowing inside me like a light bulb'.

Make a list of the similes and metaphors used in the story. Analyse their contribution to both the style and content of the narrative.

● What picture do we see of family life between the narrator, Annie and Sophie? 'Annie's a torch-bearer' (page 102). What does this further suggest about the family relationships?

● Re-read the closing paragraphs of the story. In what way does it offer a neat and satisfying conclusion? What 'patterns' and 'discoveries' have emerged and been woven together in the course of the narrative?

● Imagine that the narrator meets the man on the train at a later date and tells his own story, explaining what difference their original meeting had made to him. Write the dialogue.

● Prepare and mount a dramatised reading of the story. Try to bring out the patterns and contrasts in the narrative as well as capture the different characters and their attitudes and feelings.

● Many physically and mentally handicapped children live with their own families and attend comprehensive schools. What are your attitudes towards integrating handicapped children? Either write a story or playscript illustrating the frustrations and rewards of looking after a child with a particular handicap, *or* present a researched piece on the way the handicapped are treated by society today.

The Scythe

Before Reading

● The boy in this story moves from a city to the country. What do you think would be the major differences moving between the two? Discuss in groups any of your own personal experiences of such a change.

● What are your earliest memories? Share these in groups. Can you distinguish between events you can *actually* remember and events which you have been told about by your parents or relatives? Were there any particular people or places or incidents that stick in your mind, and for what reason?

● School offers us formal lessons of particular subjects. What 'lessons' have you learned from friends, relatives and other adults? What sorts of things are best learned informally and away from the classroom environment?

During Reading

● Look out for the ways in which Billy influences the words and deeds of the young boy.

● Note the author's attention to detail in his description of the countryside and its activities.

● There is a strong sense of nostalgia at work in the narrative. Make a note of the ways in which Ian Lumsden appears to give an 'exaggerated glow' to the past.

After Reading

● Rewrite the story in the shape of a series of diary entries made by Jim.

● In pairs consider the way in which the author has presented and structured the story. How old is the narrator now? What does he choose to tell the reader and what might he have omitted? Why does he remember the tale about the Reaper so vividly?

● Why did Billy have such an obvious effect on the young boy? Compare their friendship with that between Uncle Moro and the boy in that story (page 39). Young and old frequently come into conflict but in these two stories the 'alternate generations' have much to offer each other. Why might this be? Write your own short story which brings together a young and an old person.

● Imagine — or write from experience — that you have just moved to a new home in a different part of the country. Write about your thoughts, feelings, regrets and hopes about moving, and about your new home.

● Do you have any possessions which you clearly associate with another person? Describe them and explain the association.

● Interview an elderly friend or relative about their life and memories. Research the times they have lived through in the local history section of your local library, if this is relevant. *Either* write their biography, *or* produce a script for a radio interview with this person.

● 'The Scythe' includes very detailed 'portraits' of characters, almost as if they were strictly autobiographical. Read the following extract from Laurie Lee's well-known autobiography 'Cider With Rosie'.

'My first encounter with Uncle Ray—prospector, dynamiter, buffalo-fighter, and builder of transcontinental railways—was an occasion of memorable suddenness. One moment he was a legend at the other end of the world, the next he was in my bed. Accustomed only to the satiny bodies of my younger brothers and sister, I awoke one morning to find snoring beside me a huge and scaly man. I touched the thick legs and knotted arms and pondered the barbs on his chin, felt the crocodile flesh of this magnificent creature and wondered what it could be.

"It's your Uncle Ray come home," whispered Mother. "Get up now and let him sleep."

I saw a rust-brown face, a gaunt Indian nose, and smelt a reek of cigars and train-oil. Here was the hero of our school-boasting days, and to look on him was no disappointment. He was shiny as iron, worn as a rock, and lay like a chieftain sleeping. He'd come home on a visit from building his railways, loaded with money and thirst, and the days he spent at our house that time were full of wonder and conflagration.

For one thing he was unlike any other man we'd ever seen—or heard of, if it comes to that. With his leather-beaten face, wide teeth-crammed mouth, and far-seeing ice-blue eyes, he looked like some wigwam warrior stained with suns and heroic slaughter. He spoke the Canadian dialect of the railway camps in a drawl through his resonant nose. His body was tattooed in every quarter—ships in full sail, flags of all nations, reptiles and round-eyed maidens. By cunning flexings of his muscled flesh he could sail these ships, wave the flags in the wind, and coil snakes round the quivering girls.'

Select three older people in your family or neighbourhood. Write short but detailed and evocative descriptions of their appearance and personality.

Marriage Is A Private Affair

Before Reading

● What predictions can you make about this story from its title? Do you agree with the phrase or, given the legal aspect of marriage, is it a contradiction in terms?

● In some cultures arranged marriages are a common feature. What do you know about these? Do some research and then discuss your findings in small groups.

● Have you been in a situation where you have decided on a course of action and will not be deflected from it even though the action might have caused upset for yourself or others? Share any examples in pairs and then as a whole group. What 'lessons' emerged from people's experiences?

During Reading

● Make a note of the various male attitudes towards women shown in the story.

● Pause after, 'But years passed and that one day did not come' (page 124). How might the story continue towards some kind of resolution?

● Stop at the end of the letter from Nene — 'I shall remain here in Lagos' (page 125). Predict the last two paragraphs of the story.

After Reading

● Which of the following would you say this story is *most* to do with?
— the importance of remaining within family tradition
— the power of love
— the intensity of family relationships
— the stubborn behaviour of adults
— the problems of arranged marriages
— the healing effect of time passing.
Or would you say the focus is elsewhere? Discuss the story's central ideas in pairs and then as a whole group.

● What do we learn from this story about the nature of 'prejudice'? Compare it with other stories in this collection which have similar themes: for example, 'A Father'.

● Prepare and stage a dramatised reading of the story — complete with sound effects — which brings out the strength of family emotions that all the characters experience.

● Write a 'flashback' scene — perhaps to Nnaemeka's childhood — in which you show the powerful influence of his father and traditional family beliefs.

● Write a further exchange of letters between Nnaemeka and his father which (a) highlights their strong difference of opinion, but also (b) reflects both their wishes to find a solution.

● Imagine a sequel to 'Marriage Is A Private Affair'. Write this as a short story or a playscript.

● Draft and act out a script in which someone sticks to their principles on a matter, but finds it difficult, even painful, to do so.

● Throughout history, there have been many examples of people who have stood up strongly for, and even died for, their beliefs. Research the lives of one of these figures: for example, Joan of Arc, Thomas More, or Martin Luther King, and present a talk to your group on the subject.

Three Dreams In A Desert

Before Reading

● What is an *allegory*? Talk in groups about allegorical writing you are familiar with. Fables and morality plays offer similarities of approach.

● This story focuses on the changing role of women (and men) in the course of human history. Can you predict what particular themes the three dreams might highlight?

● Change has been constant for the human race. In groups, discuss what factors lead to change in people's *attitudes* towards one another and their lifestyles.

● *Dreams* — what associations spring to mind when you think about this word?

During Reading

● *Personification* — the presentation of an abstract quality, like freedom, in the form of a person - is a notable stylistic feature of this story. Look out for mention of inevitable necessity, mechanical invention, passion, and others.

● Make a note of how Olive Schreiner structures her story and any 'dreamlike' qualities it contains.

● Note the style of writing with its repetition of certain words and phrases, and the various Christian Bible undertones. How is your reading of this story affected by this style?

● Stop reading after, 'And he answered, "In the Future" ' (page 133). Try writing, in the author's style, a concluding six-line paragraph.

After Reading

● In pairs, discuss the style and structure of the story. Think about:
— why is it divided into sections?
— what is the time sequence within sections and for the story as a whole?
— what is the role of the narrator?
— who are the central characters?
— what is distinctive about the writing — pace, rhythm, etc.?

● Try to summarise the main ideas of 'Three Dreams In A Desert' in a paragraph of 300 words. Recast this summary in the shape of a poem or prose manifesto arguing for the emancipation of women.

● Rehearse and then produce — with music and sound effects — a dramatised reading of the story. Bring out both its dreamlike qualities and its serious underlying message.

● Olive Schreiner was born in South Africa in 1855 and died in 1920. She believed in a women's movement and wrote extensively about the necessary dignity through freedom for women. In one essay she observed, 'We have in us the blood of a womanhood that was never bought and never sold, that wore no veil, and had no foot bound, whose realised ideal of marriage was sexual companionship and an equality in duty and labour; who stood side by side with the males they loved in peace or war'.
Write a critical review of 'Three Dreams In A Desert', including discussion of:
— the phrase 'wore no veil, and had no foot bound' from the above quotation
— the historical interpretation of women's changing role offered in the story

— current debate about sexual equality
— how the story concludes.

● 'There can never be true equality between the sexes'. Debate this issue in an essay or in group discussion.

● The following is an extract from a now-celebrated speech by Dr Martin Luther King at a civil rights demonstration in Washington, USA on 28 August, 1963:

'I have a dream that one day this nation will rise up and live out the true meaning of its creed: "We hold these truths to be self-evident: that all men are created equal".

I have a dream that one day on the red hills of Georgia the sons of former slaves and the sons of former slaveowners will be able to sit down together at the table of brotherhood.

I have a dream that one day even the state of Mississippi, a state sweltering in the heat of injustice, sweltering with the heat of oppression, will be transformed into an oasis of freedom and justice.

I have a dream that my four little children will one day live in a nation where they will not be judged by the colour of their skin but by the content of their character.

I have a dream today.

I have a dream that one day down in Alabama with its vicious racists, with its governor having his lips dripping with the words of interposition and nullification, one day right there in Alabama little black boys and black girls will be able to join hands with little white boys and white girls as sisters and brothers.

I have a dream today.

I have a dream that one day every valley shall be exalted, every hill and mountain shall be made low, the rough places will be made plains, and the crooked places will be made straight, and the glory of the Lord shall be revealed, and all flesh shall see it together.

This is our hope.'

What similarities do you note between this speech and 'Three Dreams In A Desert'? Look at content and style.

Using the same stylistic devices used in both these, write your own piece of *persuasive* rhetoric. Choose a subject about which you feel strongly.

EXTENDED ASSIGNMENT

The Short Story

The telling, and memorising and writing down of short stories have been features of human life from the earliest times. It is generally accepted, however, that the short story as a *genre* (a special kind of literary work) did not establish itself until the beginning of the nineteenth century. American writers Washington Irving and Edgar Allan Poe, together with the Europeans Nicolai Gogol, Anton Chekhov and Guy de Maupassant are perhaps best known amongst the 'fathers' of the short story genre.

There have been many distinguished authors of short stories since those early days. The following quotations on the art of good storytelling are taken from a cross-section of past and present writers. Read them carefully.

'In the whole composition there should be no word written of which the tendency direct or indirect is not to the pre-established design'.   *Edgar Allan Poe*

'A short story is piece of fiction dealing with a single incident that can be read at a sitting; it is original, it must sparkle, excite and impress. It should move in an even line from its exposition to its close'.   *Somerset Maugham*

'In writing the short story it is the lines that are left out that are of paramount importance....The short story must depict more by implication than by statement, more by what is left out than left in. It ought, in fact, to resemble lace: strong but delicate, deviously woven yet full of light and air'.   *H.E.Bates*

'The writer of a short story does not travel — he is content, like an astronaut, or somebody on a package tour, to be shot to his destination; unlike the gregarious novelist, he can proceed to operate quite successfully with as few as two or three characters'.
                                                        Sean O'Faolain
'Short stories have much more in common with poetry than with novels. Partly that's because of their compactness, and the way in

which they're so tightly controlled. And partly it's because they very often only focus on a single place or moment in time'.

Linda Cookson

'What so many short stories have in common is that they are saying, in one form or another, "Isn't it strange?" They are reminding us that life, even everyday life, is more peculiar, more mysterious than we often assume'.

Graham Swift

● Read a short story by each of the writers mentioned above. Compare and contrast their differences and similarities as writers. Consult the Further Reading section on page 164. Using these and other examples, compile your own 'History of the Short Story'.

● Using the quotations above as starting-points write a critical appreciation of any three or four of the stories in *Dreams and Resolutions*. You can also use the personal essays by Linda Cookson and Giles Gordon as further background material.

● As well as telling a story, writers often want to make us think deeply about an idea or theme or issue. Make a list of the various themes raised in *Dreams And Resolutions*. Which themes do the stories have in common? Have any of the stories made you re-think your opinions or beliefs?

● Which characters in the stories in this collection did you enjoy reading about or even identify with? Write your own story centering on one of these characters, or bring together characters from different stories; for example, Babli in 'A Father' and Bev in 'He Said...'

● What are your reactions to the ways in which the stories end? Look closely at the concluding lines of each story. If you find the ending unsatisfactory, try rewriting — or acting out — an alternative one.

● When people write fiction they often do so based on something they have seen or done themselves. Which of the stories in *Dreams And Resolutions* seem to you in any way autobiographical? What clues do you look for? Write up your conclusions as a critical essay.

● 'A first reading makes you want to know what will happen; a second makes you understand why it happens; a third makes you think'. How true is this in your reading and re-reading of the stories in this collection?

Writing your own Short Story: Guidelines

● Plan out your own story by asking and answering the following questions:
— What is going to be the *subject* of the story?
— Where is it going to take place? Are there to be several different locations?
— How many characters will feature?
— Are you going to use first or third-person narration?
— Are there any particular ideas or themes you want to put across to your readers?
— Are you going to have dialogue, detailed descriptions, dialect, humour, suspense, etc?

● Think about your *audience*. Ask yourself the question, '*Who* am I writing for?'.

● A plan for writing:
— Jot down your ideas for the story.
— Sort out roughly how many paragraphs you'll need. How long will the story be?
— Write a first draft of your story. Redraft if necessary.
— Ask somebody to read it through with you. How would they make it better?
— Rewrite your final version, paying particular attention to spelling, sentences, paragraphs and appropriateness of style.
— Read it over once more to see that you haven't made any basic errors.

Good Luck!

EXTENDED ASSIGNMENT

Women And Men

The respective positions and roles of women and men come under the imaginative microscope in many of the stories in this collection. The 'battle of the sexes' is a common theme in literature and, as Olive Schreiner reveals in 'Three Dreams In A Desert', there is a long historical perspective. The following can be tackled separately or put together as an extended assignment.

● Make a list of the central female characters in three or four of the stories in this collection.

Write a brief character description of each of them.

What are their attitudes to

(a) their position in society

(b) the men they know?

What aspects of their lives would they like to change and why?

Which of the characters did you find yourself identifying with and why?

● Think about the writers in this collection and their attitudes. Would you say there are differences between the male and female writers? What are these in relation to the 'battle of the sexes'?

Does any author come across as being either anti-male or anti-female?

Which of these stories do you feel is in any way semi-autobiographical? Why?

● Using quotation, reference and comment choose four stories from this collection and discuss the subjects of:

(a) marriage

(b) romance

(c) partnership

(d) love.

● The following is an extract from the Universal Declaration of Human Rights, adopted by the United Nations Assembly in 1948:

Article 1 All human beings are born free and equal in dignity and rights. They are endowed with reason and conscience and should act towards one another in a spirit of brotherhood.

Article 2 Everyone is entitled to all rights and freedoms set forth in this Declaration, without distinction of any kind, such as race, colour, sex, language, religion, political or other opinion, national or social origin, property, birth or other status.

Article 4 No one shall be held in slavery or servitude; slavery and the slave trade shall be prohibited in all their forms.

Article 16 men and women of full age, without any limitation due to race, nationality or religion, have the right to marry and to found a family. They are entitled to equal rights as to marriage, during marriage and at its dissolution. Marriage shall be entered into only with free and full consent of the intending spouses.'

In what ways are these 'entitlements' observed or challenged in the stories in *Dreams And Resolutions*? Write a controversial essay on the subject. Refer in your essay to the extract from Martin Luther King on page 156.

● Research and present as a project *either* 'The Role of Women in Society Today' *or* 'The Historical Role of Women in Society'. Discussion of the following might be helpful:
— presentation of women in literature
— treatment by society of women writers
— women in different cultures
— Suffragette Movement
— the work of the Equal Opportunities Commission
— education of girls
— attitudes of the media towards women
— changing attitudes amongst men
— new employment patterns and opportunities
— progress in birth control.

EXTENDED ASSIGNMENT

Meetings

The Irish author James Joyce wrote a celebrated collection of short stories titled *Dubliners*. In each of the stories characters experience what he called 'a moment of epiphany'. In other words, something happens to a character which changes their views or outlook on life and people. In *Dreams And Resolutions* every story contains some kind of meeting or confrontation which has an effect on one of the characters. Flannery O'Connor's story is a particularly striking example in which all three protagonists will have been deeply affected by their chance encounter.

● Make a list of the different 'meetings' in these stories.
What is the location of each?
Who is involved?
What is the effect of the meeting on the characters? Is it for better or worse?
Write up your findings in a critical review.

● Why does someone behave in the way they do? What causes them to take one line of action rather than another? What motivates the characters in these stories? Working in groups, choose one of the stories. Then take it in turns to play the part of one of the characters. Each character is placed in the witness-box and quizzed by the others as to why they behaved as they did in the story. You might start with 'Three Resolutions To One Kashmiri Encounter' or 'Sphinxes'.

● 'Fireflies' uses the first-person 'I' narrator to tell the story, while 'The Life You Save May Be Your Own' has a third-person narrator observing the action from outside. In conveying the impact of 'meetings', what do you think are the disadvantages and advantages of the different types of narrative standpoint? Discuss this issue in pairs and then in small groups. What conclusions have you come to? Are your sympathies with characters affected by the type of narrator?

● Write your own story or playscript in which you bring together characters from different stories to meet one another. What might happen, for example, if Mr Shiftlet encountered Mr Hovsepian? Use the detail of the original stories to provide you with clues as to characterisation.

● At the end of a short story we as readers are left with a series of images, snapshots of people's lives. Imagine you could interview any of the characters on a television chat show. Write the script in which you ask them to reflect on the 'meeting' they had and what impact it had on their lives. A good starting-point might be with the girl in 'A Drive In The Country' or with the narrator in 'Fireflies'.

EXTENDED ASSIGNMENT

Prejudice

Prejudice is all about *pre*-judging people and things. How often have you heard at home, at school, at a club, or on television, someone say that they don't like a place they have never seen, a type of food they have never tasted, a language they have not heard or a person they have never really talked to? But it is also more than just that! The occurence of different *forms* of prejudice is so frequent in our daily lives that it is hardly surprising writers have chosen to explore its roots and effects in short stories, poetry, novels and plays. The authors in *Dreams And Resolutions* are no exception.

● If we look through the stories in thes collection we find the following kinds of prejudice:

'Three Resolutions To One Kashmiri Encounter': the prejudice of a tourist towards a 'beggar'.

'The Life You Save May Be Your Own': the prejudice of one man towards a simple girl.

'A Drive In The Country': the prejudice of a young woman towards her parents.

'Talks With My Uncle Moro': the prejudice of the townspeople towards an itinerant farmworker, and the *lack* of prejudice towards him from the young boy.

'A Father': the prejudice of parents against their daughter's lifestyle and personal choices.

'Sphinxes': the prejudice of 'The Man In The Brown Jacket' towards 'foreigners'.

Extend and continue the list, making a note of both the presence *and* the absence of prejudice. Analyse the *types* of prejudice explored in the stories and any explanations of root causes offered by the authors. Write up your conclusions in a critical essay on the topic, using quotation, reference and comment.

● In small groups and then as a whole group, discuss the following:
 — What are the roots of prejudice in society?
 — What examples of prejudice do we see in our immediate environment?
 — What can we do to combat our own and other people's prejudices?
 — Thinking about the extracts from the Universal Declaration of Human Rights (page 160) and from Martin Luther King (page 156), what progress would we say has taken place in the recent past in the way of reducing prejudice?
 — Does the final line of 'Three Dreams In A Desert' suggest there are no final solutions?

● Imagine you have the opportunity to interview any of the characters for a magazine article that you are putting together on the topic of Prejudice. What questions would you ask? What might their responses be? Write the interview you have and then the finished article, complete with quotations and a commentary which includes your own values and opinions.

*F*urther *R*eading

This is necessarily a selective list, featuring short stories which students in the 14–17 age range will find accessible in both subject matter and language. Many of the themes and ideas present in *Dreams And Resolutions* can be revisited in the following collections and selections.

Short Stories from India, Pakistan and Bangladesh, ed. Ranjana Ash, Harrap (1980)

Gorilla My Love, Toni Cade Bambara, The Women's Press (1984)

The Seabirds Are Still Alive, Toni Cade Bambara, The Women' Press (1984)

The Poison Ladies and Other Stories, H.E. Bates, Wheaton (1976)

Somerset Maugham Short Stories, ed. Roy Blatchford, Longman (1986)

The Stories of Ronald Blythe, Chatto & Windus (1985)

The Threshing Floor, Barbara Burfood, Sheba (1986)

Stories of John Cheever, Penguin (1982)

Portraits, Kate Chopin, The Women's Press (1979)

After The Fountain, Linda Cookson, Cassells (1988)

Poona Company, Farrukh Dhondy, Collins (1980)

Selected Stories, Nadine Gordimer, Penguin (1983)

Southern African Stories, ed. Stephen Gray, Penguin (1985)

Collected Short Stories, Graham Greene, Penguin (1986)

The Open Road, Jennifer Gubb, Onlywomen Press (1984)

A Bit Of Singing And Dancing, Susan Hill, Penguin (1975)

British Short Stories Of Today, ed. Esmor Jones, Penguin (1987)

Dubliners, James Joyce, Penguin

Merle and Other Stories, Paule Marshall, Virago (1985)

The Water's Edge, Moy McCrory, Sheba (1985)

Stories of the Waterfront, John Morrison, Penguin (1984)

Darkness, Bharati Mukherjee, Penguin (1985)

A Flag On The Island, V.S. Naipaul, Penguin (1969)

A Sense Of Shame, Jan Needle, Collins (1982)

A Good Man Is Hard To Find, Flannery O'Connor, The Women's Press (1980)

My Oedipus Complex, Frank O'Connor, Penguin (1984)

Foreign Affairs and Other Stories, Sean O'Faolain, Penguin (1986)

Collected Stories of John O'Hara, Pan (1986)

Collected Short Stories, James Plunkett, Poolbeg Press (1977)

More To Life Than Mr Right, ed. Rosemary Stones, Collins (198)

Learning to Swim and Other Stories, Graham Swift, Picador (1985)

You Can't Keep a Good Woman Down, Alice Walker, The Women's Press (1982)

In Love and Trouble, Alice Walker, The Women's Press (1984)

Further Reading

Collected Stories of Eudora Welty, Penguin (1983)
Passion Fruit, ed. Jeanette Winterson, Pandora, Unwin Hyman (1986)

*A*cknowledgements

The editor and publishers would like to express thanks to the following for permission to reproduce personal essays and stories in this collection:

Linda Cookson and Giles Gordon for their personal essays, contributed specially for this collection.

'Three Resolutions To One Kashmiri Encounter' © Giles Gordon 1981: reprinted by permission of the author. First published in *Scottish Short Stories*: 1981, Collins.
'The Life You Save May Be Your Own' © Flannery O'Connor: A D Peters & Co. Ltd.
'A Drive In The Country' © Graham Greene: Laurence Pollinger Limited. First published in *Collected Stories*, Heinemann and Bodley Head.
'Talks With My Uncle Moro' © Geoffrey Dean: Longman Cheshire (Australia). Originally published in *Cold Dead, Monday and other Australian Short Stories*.
'A Father' © Bharati Mukherjee: Penguin Books Ltd.
'Sphinxes' © Philip First, 1986: Maggie Noach Literary Agency. First published in *Paper Thin and other Stories*, Paladin.
'He Said...' © Barbara Burford: Sheba Publishers. First published in *The Threshing Floor*.
'Fireflies' © Linda Cookson: reprinted by permission of the author. First published in *After The Fountain*, Cassell, 1988.
'The Scythe' © Ian Lumsden: reprinted by permission of the author.
'Marriage Is A Private Affair' © Chinua Achebe 1972: David Bolt Associates. First published in *Girls At War and other Stories*, Heinemann Educational.
'Three Dreams In A Desert' by Olive Schreiner is out of copyright.

Unwin Hyman English Series

Series editor: Roy Blatchford
Advisers: Jane Leggett and Gervase Phinn

Unwin Hyman Short Stories

Openings   edited by Roy Blatchford
Round Two   edited by Roy Blatchford
School's OK   edited by Josie Karavasil and Roy Blatchford
Stepping Out   edited by Jane Leggett
That'll Be The Day   edited by Roy Blatchford
Sweet and Sour   edited by Gervase Phinn
It's Now or Never   edited by Jane Leggett and Roy Blatchford
Pigs Is Pigs   edited by Trevor Millum
Snakes and Ladders   edited by H.T. Robertson
Crying For Happiness   edited by Jane Leggett

Unwin Hyman Collections

Free As I Know   edited by Beverley Naidoo
Solid Ground   edited by Jane Leggett and Sue Libovitch
In Our Image   edited by Andrew Goodwyn

Unwin Hyman Plays

Stage Write   edited by Gervase Phinn